MW01138776

THE MURDER NEXT DOOR

Mrs. Lillywhite Investigates
BOOK TWO

EMILY QUEEN

The Murder Next Door

ISBN- 978-1-953044-22-8

First Edition

Printed in the U.S.A.

Table of Contents

CHAPTER ONE

Rosemary Lillywhite scowled and flung yet another dress into a rapidly growing discard pile, noting with frustration that her wardrobe was nearly as empty as her suitcase. In a weak moment, she had allowed her dearest friend, Vera, to clear out anything she considered too somber. Since then, she'd deftly avoided Vera's rabid attempts to drag her into the dress shops. However, faced with the task of packing for a holiday in Cyprus, Rosemary's sense of victory had evaporated.

With a sigh, she flipped the lid of the case closed and paced the breadth of her bedroom. Since she would not be embarking on this trip alone, she knew she could rely upon Vera to rally to the occasion and bring along more than enough clothing for them both.

With that settled, her thoughts wandered back in the direction they had been taking ever since her brother, Frederick, had announced his choice of traveling companion. It wasn't as though Frederick had intended to make Rosemary uncomfortable by inviting Desmond Cooper along; after all, young girls tended not to share their secrets with their older brothers, particularly when those secrets involved a case of heart-wrenching, unrequited puppy love.

Of course, Rosemary was no longer an awkward twelve-year-old girl, and she hadn't given her brother's childhood pal a second thought since the moment she'd met Andrew Lillywhite—the man who would become her husband and the love of her life.

Except, Andrew had passed away almost a year before, and just the idea of spending time with someone about whom she'd once enjoyed romantic daydreams made her feel as though she were betraying his memory.

You're not betraying anyone, and Andrew would want you to be happy. Rosemary could hear Vera's voice in her head as clearly as if her friend had been whispering in her ear, and she sighed.

It didn't matter anyway because Rosemary had no intention of finding herself still attracted to Desmond Cooper. She hoped he'd grown some sort of hump or that he had begun to go prematurely bald—anything to put a nail in the coffin of her childhood crush. What Rosemary wanted was a healthy dose of sun, sand, and seawater—and a chance to forget her troubles, even if only for a couple of weeks.

The main attraction of the holiday rested in Rosemary's desire to get away from the city of London—and not for a quick jaunt in the countryside, but somewhere even further where nobody knew her as a poor, lonely widow. It was more than just an indulgent whim; it was something she needed to do for the sake of her own sanity.

Aside from the fact that she'd lost her husband,

Rosemary was haunted by other ghosts she'd prefer to leave at home. Just a few weeks prior, she'd been involved in a murder investigation after finding a dead body at a party she'd attended near her parents' country house in the village of Pardington. Since then, she'd been in a sort of limbo state, wondering what to do with her life and whether her calling was art, as she'd always believed, or if she was meant for something different—something entirely unprecedented for a woman.

While Rosemary's mind wandered to and fro, she tuned out all the noise around her. Gertrude, the cook, prepared for supper by pounding a piece of veal into submission with all the tenderness of a workman swinging a sledgehammer. The housekeeper's broom swished back and forth across the corridor floor, its swipes punctuated by the heavy thump of her footsteps. Rosemary's maid, Anna, kept a running commentary with the butler, Wadsworth, as he did whatever it was that butlers did, discussing the details of the forthcoming holiday. All these sounds of the household below her moving in its undulating rhythm turned to a background too indistinct to pierce her thoughts.

All of this Rosemary missed, and she might have also missed the sound of angry voices if she hadn't tripped over one of the hangers she'd haphazardly thrown aside and found herself nearly kissing the floor.

One wall of her bedroom butted up against the parlor of the adjacent townhouse, and the most Rosemary had ever heard were the muted notes of soft jazz that occasionally lulled her to sleep. Until recently, anyway, when other rumblings had become more frequent.

Pushing herself up from the floor, Rosemary leaned a little closer to the wall because, well, nobody was around to chide her for eavesdropping, and she was as curious as any other person in the world. It mattered little because all she heard was the sound of raised voices, both male and female, followed by the distant slamming of a door and then a short, muffled spate of crying.

Soft of heart, Rosemary wished for a way to offer comfort without intruding on her neighbor's privacy or, worse, without seeming like a busybody. What did one say in those circumstances? Rosemary couldn't think of the proper etiquette for knocking on the door of an acquaintance to pry into her affairs.

Still, being merely neighbors hadn't stopped Abigail from bringing round a platter of cakes or a plate of supper every evening for a fortnight after Andrew passed away. Realizing now that she'd not taken the time to thank the woman for her kindness, Rosemary felt a debt was owed and that the time to repay it had come.

Knowing she ought to return to the task at hand but accepting that her curious mind wouldn't be content if she didn't at least attempt to find out what was going on next door, Rosemary sighed. With a wry expression on her heart-shaped face, she descended the stairs and made her way onto the front doorstep.

Number 8 Park Road, where Rosemary lived above her late husband's private investigative office, was situated one house down from the corner lot where Dr. and Mrs. Redberry resided. Their doorstep stood just beside Rosemary's, but unlike Number 8, the neighboring townhouse bordered two streets and featured an entirely separate entrance to the ground-floor office where Dr. Redberry tended his dental patients.

As fate would have it, Mrs. Redberry sat on the steps with her head in her hands, partially hidden by an enormous hydrangea bush. Steeling herself, Rosemary prepared to overstep the boundaries of neighborly decorum by poking her nose into business that was none of her concern.

How could she simply walk away from someone in obvious pain, though? Especially when the woman had been nothing but kind to her during the years they'd shared a wall.

"Abigail, are you quite well?" Rosemary asked, poking her head around the wrought-iron handrail and casting a sympathetic look in the woman's direction.

Startled, Abigail turned wide, red-rimmed eyes Rosemary's way and attempted to collect herself. "I'm fine, thank you." She replied with a sniffle and a forced smile.

Like hell you are, Rosemary thought to herself, but said gently, "You don't look fine to me. Sometimes it helps to talk to someone, and I have found that the most receptive audiences are often people you wouldn't have expected."

Perhaps, in her preoccupation with her own troubles, she'd overlooked a possible friend. Abigail Redberry wasn't much older than Rosemary herself, and judging by her simple sunflower-colored dress and makeup-free face, they might actually have a lot in common.

"I just … I don't know … I'm at a loss, to be perfectly honest," Abigail finally said with a sigh. Her face began to scrunch up again, and it took a visible effort for her to regain her composure. "Martin and I have never argued like this before. I thought we had the perfect marriage. I've known the man since we were children, but lately, I'm never certain where we stand. The smallest things set off his temper, and he has been—" Abigail paused as though catching herself before revealing too much and then continued. "He is not the gentle man I once knew."

Rosemary sat down on the step beside Abigail and rested her chin in the palm of her hand. "What seems to be the problem, if you don't mind my asking?"

Abigail shook her head. "I find myself somewhat embarrassed to say, but I bought a rather expensive dress for the theater tonight—at Martin's request, mind you—but when the check came, he was furious." Her almond-shaped eyes widened again, and she clapped a hand over her mouth. "I shouldn't have told you that. He'd kill me if he knew I had discussed our finances with a virtual stranger."

"I assure you, Abigail, I won't breathe a word to anyone. And we're not exactly strangers. We're neighbors, and by all rights, we should have become friends long ago," Rosemary declared. Furthermore, she felt a sense of conviction, as the words were leaving her lips, that they were true.

Face brightening, Abigail nodded once and put on a stiff upper lip. "It will all come right. I'm overreacting, of course. Martin is under a great deal of strain with his work. There's a dentist over on the high street who has been trying to steal his patients right out from under him. I believe he's worried about our livelihood, though I expect it's just a minor storm, and everything will come right in the end." She repeated the statement as if saying it over and over might make it true.

Laying a gentle hand on Abigail's arm, Rosemary said, "I'm sure it will, and you let me know if you need anything. I have a willing ear and a dry shoulder to cry on." Just in time, she remembered to add, "Though I'm sorry to say I'll be on holiday for the next few weeks. When I get back, why don't we have lunch?"

"Thank you, Rosemary. Really. It means a lot, and I feel better already. I should go prepare Martin's tea tray. He'll be ready for it soon." Abigail bade her goodbye and retreated into her home with a bit more spring in her step than Rosemary imagined she'd walked outdoors with.

The conversation with Abigail reminded Rosemary of her own husband, and the memory brought both pain and gratitude. Andrew had rarely ever raised a voice to his wife, and he certainly wouldn't have begrudged her the right to speak to her friends about any marital issue they might have had. She thought Dr. Redberry sounded like a cad but wouldn't have dared express her opinion aloud, at least not to his wife.

And that was part of why she feared she would never again find a man to love. Andrew had been a diamond in the rough, and it was unlikely any other man would ever compare. Rosemary let the thought slide right back out of her head. She had no intention of allowing anyone to try anytime soon, regardless, and ignored the voice in the back of her mind that kept whispering Desmond's name in her ear.

CHAPTER TWO

Rosemary walked back in the direction she'd come, sat down on her own front doorstep, and leaned back on her palms while the sun shone down on her upturned face. Winter had been intolerably long that year, and her first holidays without Andrew had taken their toll.

Now that summer's heat had returned, Rosemary wanted to soak up as much of it as she could. It was almost as though she had awakened from a terrible nightmare, and even though she still mourned, the fear and the pain and the dread of it all had begun to dissipate.

"Excuse me, Miss Rose." Anna appeared in the doorway with a large tin cradled in one hand. "Cook has made up a batch of boiled sweets for the trip. She said to tell you she used a special recipe and added plenty of ginger as a remedy for seasickness. Shall I put them in the black valise or the brown one?"

Wrinkling her nose, Rosemary replied, "I'd greatly prefer you to wrap them in brown paper and drop them in the nearest bin. I absolutely cannot abide the flavor of ginger." Looking over her shoulder, Rosemary took in

Anna's pinched expression and assessed her maid's mood as fearful. Cook could be formidable when she got an idea in her head. "Though I suppose we could offer them to Vera. She has a passion for the warmer spices."

"Yes, Miss Rose," Normally talkative, Anna seemed somewhat sober, and Rosemary wondered if there was something troubling her maid. Before she could ask, Anna hurried back inside.

As though thinking of her friend had summoned her, a town car pulled up to the curb and had barely come to a full stop before Vera veritably bounced from the rear door. "Rosie, dear!" she called, sashaying across the footway to kiss her friend on both cheeks. "You're positively glowing. I told you a little sun would do you some good. I simply cannot wait to sink my toes into the sand. Have Frederick and his little friend arrived yet? Or am I the first and best prepared?"

Vera fired off questions without waiting for Rosemary to answer, a habit Rosemary had long since stopped chiding her for and simply accepted as an immutable facet of her personality.

"Of course not. You remember the way he and Desmond were as children, don't you? Always chasing metaphorical butterflies—and oftentimes, real ones. I imagine they've found themselves embroiled in some outrageous pursuit yet again and won't arrive until the final second. Or, they're skulking behind the rose bushes, listening to our conversation." Rosemary peered around her with a raised eyebrow to illustrate her point; she was only half kidding, and wouldn't have been at all surprised if her joke was entirely correct.

Vera laughed and instructed her driver to unload her

luggage from the boot of the car just as Wadsworth opened the front door of the townhouse. "Miss Vera, it's a pleasure to see you, as always." Rosemary's butler had a soft spot for her best friend, even though Vera enjoyed teasing him as often as possible. Had she been anyone else, Wadsworth would have given her his version of the evil eye, but even he could not resist Vera's charms. As if many men had ever dared to try.

"And you as well," Vera said, allowing him to take her hand and give it a gentle squeeze before handling the luggage. "If you're not careful, Rose, I'll steal this fine specimen away from you." She winked at Rosemary behind Wadsworth's back.

Rosemary grinned. "I'm not worried. Your flat is far smaller than my townhouse. The poor man would be bored inside of an afternoon."

Tossing her head, Vera retorted in her loftiest tone, "My flat is fabulous, as you well know. What would I do with more space? I'm only one person, after all." The color drained from her face as she realized she might have made an enormous gaffe. Rosemary hadn't intended to live alone; she had expected to have started a family by now. "I'm sorry, Rosie, I didn't mean anything by that."

"Don't apologize, Vera, for goodness' sake. I appreciate the sentiment, but I'm not made of glass. At least, not anymore."

Vera said nothing but gave her friend a reassuring pat on the hand. "I know, Rosie, but I'm still sorry. My mouth often runs without the benefit of my brain being engaged."

"You know my invitation to come live here with me

still stands, don't you?" Rosemary ignored the apology and instead homed in on the more pressing concern. Vera's point was valid. Rosemary practically rattled around in the townhouse all alone, and she wouldn't mind the intrusion. In fact, it might give her something else upon which to focus.

"I do," Vera said slowly, "and I'm seriously considering the prospect. Why don't we see how this holiday goes, and then decide? You might discover that my annoying habits have worsened rather than improved since our school days."

"Of that, I have no doubt." Rosemary softened the criticism with a smile and added, "Just as I'm certain all your positive attributes far outshine the bad, and even if they didn't, I wouldn't care a jot." She hoped there wasn't another reason for Vera's reluctance, but didn't have time to dwell on the subject because just then, another car pulled to the curb.

Without even realizing she was doing it, Rosemary held her breath and smoothed her hair. Her actions did not, however, escape Vera's notice. Whether she knew it or not—and Vera believed she did, deep down—Rosemary was excited to see Desmond after all these years, and Vera intended to thoroughly enjoy watching the show.

Frederick exited first and tossed a dazzling grin in Rosemary's direction. A lock of golden hair the same shade as hers fell into his eyes, and he brushed it aside absently while making a beeline for his sister. He scooped her up into a hug and swung her around until she giggled.

"Put me down, Freddie! Right this instant!" But there

was no sting to her words. For that, he was grateful, since the playful mood seemed more like her old self. Frederick hoped the time away from London would bring back even more of her vigor.

Rosemary might have known her brother to be full of mischievous intent, but she had been wrong in her assumption that Frederick hadn't brought Desmond along in an attempt to unnerve her. She had believed Frederick clueless regarding her girlish infatuation with the man, but she'd underestimated the amount of attention brothers pay to their younger sisters. Now, Frederick had Rosemary right where he wanted her and, like Vera, couldn't help but wonder what would happen when she came face-to-face with Desmond.

For both of them, it was a little bit of a letdown, because Rosemary had got quite used to hiding her emotions. On the inside, however, her heartbeat quickened while she held her breath and waited for Desmond to emerge from the back seat of the car.

When he unfolded himself and rose to his full six feet, two inches topped by a mop of curly, chestnut hair, Rosemary's hopes fell to ruin. By the look of it, there was little to no chance of Desmond going bald anytime soon, and neither had he grown an unsightly hump. There he stood, a dashing man with sparkling hazel eyes and a set of full lips over an impossibly straight row of teeth. In short, he could get a woman thoroughly syncopated with little effort.

"Rosemary Woolridge, as I live and breathe," he said with a wide grin, striding the short distance between them and enveloping Rosemary in another hug, this one gentle and friendly rather than rib-shattering like

Frederick's.

"Hello, Desmond. You look well." The understatement of the year, but all Rosemary could manage. She didn't even bother to correct his misuse of her maiden name.

Desmond smiled down at her. "As do you." He winked at Rosemary, raising a blush to her cheeks, and deposited a kiss on her outstretched hand before turning his attention to Vera. "I see you're still keeping deplorable company."

The two stared one another down through slitted lids—it seemed that the men who didn't fall for Vera's spectacular good looks and charming personality tended to regard her as rather a handful. The standoff ended when Vera deadpanned, "I can still take you, Desmond dear. Don't let the heels fool you."

He laughed, and the ice was broken. What's more, the heat had dissipated from Rosemary's face, and for that, she was grateful. Her color had returned to normal, and she'd already forced the memory of the butterflies in her stomach out of her mind and deep into her subconscious.

"Wadsworth will handle your bags and take them up to the guest rooms. Vera will stay with me. We leave tomorrow by the four o'clock train."

"Which leaves us the evening. Quite enough time to get good and sozzled, huh, Des?" Frederick elbowed his friend in the ribs and wiggled his eyebrows as he followed Rosemary up the steps to the front doorstep.

Desmond shook his head, ruefully. "Not all of us can handle your level of drinking, old friend. But I won't say no to a night on the town. How about it, ladies?"

"Actually," Rosemary said, "we have tickets to a

show this evening, and Vera is demanding the two of you accompany us." She cast a sideways glance in Vera's direction. "As moral support."

Frederick peered at Vera curiously. "I've never known Vera's morals to be in want of support, scant as they are. What gives?"

"None of your business, Frederick," Vera snapped.

"Come, Vera, we can't expect them to go to war blindly. Not without at least giving them the lay of the land first," Rosemary admonished.

"Fine," Vera huffed. "If you must know, I was up for a part in the production, but that miserable Jennie Bryer stole the role right out from under me. Now, I feel it is my duty to attend the premiere and heckle her to my heart's content. I assume I can count on you two fools for some shameless ill behavior?"

She stalked into the front parlor without a backward glance, as she needed not a whit of reassurance that her wishes would be honored. "And if either one of you breathes a word about how beautiful she is, I swear you will regret it for the rest of your days."

Both Frederick and Desmond knew from experience how seriously Vera took such promises and made a solemn vow not to ogle Jennie Bryer overmuch. Rosemary smirked to herself, sure the venture would never go off as planned, and amused at the thought of what form Vera's retribution might take.

CHAPTER THREE

"Now," Desmond slouched on Rosemary's parlor settee, and gestured with his after-dinner aperitif, a G&T with more gin than tonic, "I want to hear how you're faring these days, Rosie? I was very sorry to hear about your husband, and even more sorry to have been traveling and unable to attend the funeral." He paused as if a thought had just occurred to him, and then flushed. "Maybe I shouldn't have brought it up."

"Don't trouble yourself, and thank you for asking," Rosemary said with a wave of her hand. "I'm doing much better now. Of course, it comes in waves, but that's the nature of these things. At this very moment, I couldn't be happier. I'm surrounded by caring friends, and I'm looking forward to our holiday abroad. Will this be your first time to visit Cyprus, or have you been there before?"

Desmond nodded. "I have, yes. Once, and I'm looking forward to a return visit. Very relaxing place. What more could anyone ask than sand, sun, and beautiful mountains? I hope you two will come on a hike with Freddie and me."

Rosemary looked to Vera, who smiled thinly. "Luring Vera off the beach might be a chore, but if I can manage, you may count us in," she said wryly. "What have you been up to the past few years, Des? All Frederick ever tells us is that you've been gallivanting around the world and that you spent some time in the States."

"He *would* call it gallivanting." Desmond shot his friend a withering look, and then returned his gaze to Rosemary. "I call it quite something else entirely," he continued with a charming grin. "In pursuit of the lion's share of my great-aunt's inheritance, my father insisted upon my squiring her from one end of the world to the other. I hardly remember what it's like to not live out of a steamer trunk these days."

A short moment of silence followed the admission, and then Vera trilled out a laugh. "Around the world in eighty days with a maiden aunt. Sounds like a lukewarm adventure if ever there was one. Tell me, did it pay off? Did she decide to cut you in on scads of ready money when she toddles off into the next life?"

Frowning at Vera, Desmond admitted, "If you must know, after I got over feeling like a trained dog sent to fetch a bone, I came to quite like the old girl. I shall miss her when she goes, but I rather consider I've done my familial duty."

Feeling warmly towards him, Rosemary said, "That's quite interesting, Des. You will have to tell us all about it when we're in Cyprus with nothing to do but lounge around and relax."

Desmond laughed. "It may be interesting, but it's nothing compared to solving a murder! Frederick told me about your exploits in Pardington, and I have to say,

I'm impressed and intrigued. How did you figure out who killed that poor sod?"

Rosemary cast an appreciative gaze towards Vera. "The killer slipped up and tried to pin the caper on poor Frederick. None of us fancied him taking a ride on the end of a noose, so we put our heads together, and the rest was just a bit of quick thinking."

"The moral of that story, my good man, is to avoid getting spifflicated and sleeping in the rough when someone's plotting dirty deeds and trying to lay them on you." As Rosemary expected, Frederick evidenced no chagrin. "If not for our Rosemary, I'd be but a fond memory by now."

Vera insisted on being acknowledged for her contribution to the solving of the crime, and a short but friendly discussion ensued until Rosemary had had enough.

"I think it's about time we dressed for the theater, don't you, Vera?" Rosemary asked. Vera looked at the clock and jumped up from her chair.

"Where did the time go? We've just over an hour to powder our noses and shrug on the glad rags. That's cutting it close," she said and pulled Rosemary towards the parlor door.

Rosemary went to pull the door closed behind her, but paused when Desmond, apparently thinking she was out of earshot, spoke to Frederick.

"She seems to be doing quite well, all things considered," Desmond commented thoughtfully.

Her brother grunted. "She puts on a good show, and this is certainly better than the catatonic state she was in just after Andrew passed away. I'd like to believe she's moving on with her life, but I can't say for sure. That's part of why I wanted to accompany her to Cyprus. Mother and Father agreed that it would be best if I went along, and since work has become quite a chore, I jumped at the chance."

Rosemary clicked the door shut silently, unsure whether she was glad to have people concerned for her, or irritated that they felt the need to supervise her.

"So?" Vera flopped down onto Rosemary's bed and looked at her friend expectantly. "Does Desmond measure up to the memories you had of him, or is he looking a little long in the tooth nowadays?"

Rosemary cast her a wry glance. "You know good and well that's not the case. You do have eyes, after all. If it's possible, he looks even better than he did back then. Less boy, more man, I suppose."

"Right, Rosie, but did he make you feel anything? Did you get the butterflies?" Vera prodded.

Rosemary contemplated the question. Vera would accept nothing less than total honesty from her best friend. "Yes, I suppose you could say something took flight, but I think it was simply a nostalgic figment of my imagination."

Whether Rosemary thought she was being honest or not, Vera didn't buy the line for a second.

"Yes, well, I suppose we'll see, won't we? A few weeks in Cyprus will give you more than enough time to tell if you like him."

"I already know I like him, Vera, but that doesn't mean I want to be handcuffed to him. I'm still not ready, and you know it. Involving Desmond now would be putting the cart before the horse."

"At least it's a stallion, Rose, and they're rarer than a unicorn these days. All I ask is that you give him a chance," Vera implored, even if her words fell on deaf ears. She wasn't trying to be insensitive; it simply broke her heart to still see occasional traces of sadness in her friend's eyes, and she missed the lighthearted, perpetually smiling woman Rosemary had always been.

Rosemary scoffed. "It doesn't only matter what I think of him. He may not find me at all attractive, you know."

"And you don't seem to notice the way men look at you. You never have. It's not one of your more redeeming qualities," Vera retorted. "Modesty can only take one so far."

Setting her lips against the smirk that wanted to surface, Rosemary merely sought to mollify her. "Of course, Vera. Whatever you say."

While Rosemary stood under Vera's fiery glare, Anna walked into the room carrying an armful of freshly laundered clothing. She didn't say a word but juggled the load onto her other arm while she straightened up Rosemary's dressing table. After a moment, she seemed to notice Vera.

"Oh, hello, Miss Vera. You look lovely," Anna said, though her eyes darted around the room while she shifted from one foot to the other.

Rosemary raised a brow. "Are you quite all right, Anna?" she asked with genuine concern. Scatterbrained was not a word she would have used to describe her maid, at least under normal circumstances.

"What? Oh, yes, yes, I'm fine, nothing to worry

about." Anna looked down and started, as if noticing the bundle she carried for the first time. "I'd just lose my head today if it wasn't attached." She resumed puttering about, setting things to rights, and then stopped dead in her tracks as if she'd forgotten what she'd intended to do.

"You clearly aren't fine, Anna," Rosemary pressed. "Whatever it is, you can talk to me about it." Anna was a good maid and a fine girl. Not much more than a teenager, she'd been in Rosemary's employ for several years, and they had shared a closer relationship than was typical between a servant and mistress. In fact, the term 'mistress' was one Rosemary preferred not to use, and the sentiment behind her choice was part of what made her different from other employers.

Still, Anna simply gave her a wan smile. "I'm just feeling a little frazzled, that's all. Nothing to worry about, I'll be right as rain and ready for our travels, don't you worry." Frazzled was an understatement, Rosemary thought when Anna brushed off her concern once more.

She let it go, and allowed Anna to beat a hasty retreat, but vowed to speak with the girl and dig out the problem at her earliest opportunity.

CHAPTER FOUR

"An evening of boring theater was not what I had in mind when I said I'd like a night on the town, you know," Desmond complained as he topped off his glass of gin with a splash of tonic and a squeeze of lime. "I never did enjoy the Bard as much as my teachers thought I ought to. Downright depressing, old Shakespeare, wasn't he?" He leaned over the bar cart and tilted his head towards her.

Rosemary tilted her head to one side. "*A Midsummer Night's Dream* is a comedy. How can you not enjoy a story filled with fairies and lovers and beautiful poetry?"

He lifted a shoulder carelessly. "I'm male, I suppose. That's my only defense. We aren't always attuned to the finer nuances and tend to prefer our love stories off the page. Or off the stage, as it may be."

Being quintessentially male, he proved the point by missing the subtle roll of Rosemary's eyes towards the heavens, though he gave her a smile that smoothed over the gaffe. Tonight, she thought, was not a night for pointing out the glaring differences between male and female sensibilities.

She dragged her attention away from his dimples and back to the words he was speaking.

"You certainly do look lovely, Rosemary. You'd fit right in with the fairies of Shakespeare's imagination."

She had to admit, she felt better in the deep-purple silk dress than she had in unrelieved widow's black, especially since she knew it set off her golden hair and complemented her figure. Not carefree, exactly, but far better than she had in ages.

She blushed, and took a swig of her drink to avoid replying immediately, and then decided to accept the compliment without worrying whether it might mean anything. "Thank you, Desmond."

Rosemary was grateful when Vera and Frederick swept into the parlor and drew the attention away from her, and she didn't even bat an eyelash at their squabbling. She supposed she might as well get used to it. Two weeks with the pair of them acting like children would drive her mad unless she maintained her sense of humor.

"It was Clifford Leighton," Frederick insisted. "He bragged about it for weeks."

Vera stopped, turned, and wagged a finger under Frederick's nose. "You're all wet. It was Jonty Emsworth, and that's the final word on the subject."

Rather than backing down, Frederick thrust his face closer to Vera's. "Clifford Leighton," he enunciated each syllable.

Stretching up on her toes, Vera matched his fervor. "Jonty, and he did a right good job of it, too."

"It was not."

"Was too."

This went on for several more turns until Rosemary couldn't help but intervene.

"Here now, what's this all about?"

So close their noses nearly touched and without taking her eyes off Frederick, Vera snapped, "Your brother is under the misguided notion that Clifford Leighton was the boy with whom I shared my first kiss." Then she called Frederick a name that no lady would repeat in polite company.

As she had done in the past, Rosemary dearly wished the sparks between Frederick and Vera carried even a hint of romantic feeling. As vehemently as they argued, she thought they'd love one another even more so. Alas, it was not to be, and the insults grew increasingly scandalous until Rosemary couldn't hold back her laughter.

"You're fools, both of you," she said between giggles, "and wrong besides. Vera's first kiss was with Basil Harrington at the church fete the year we turned twelve. She gave him a boiled sweet, and he rewarded her with a peck on the lips. Then his ears turned red, and he had to go to confession."

Vera's sour mood popped like a soap bubble, and her silvery laugh rang out. "I'd forgotten. He had to say ten Hail Marys, and he didn't speak to me again for a month."

Turning to Frederick, Vera couldn't resist a final taunt. "You were still wrong."

"So were you," came his retort.

"Come now, you two. We are all adults here, are we not?" Desmond intervened while Rosemary convulsed with silent laughter.

"It's a losing battle, Des. I promise you. Just bring plenty of cotton to stuff in your ears while we're in Cyprus. Trust me; you'll need the relief," Rosemary sputtered while she tried to catch her breath.

Desmond shrugged and sat down on one of the armchairs, crossed his legs, and watched while Rosemary tried to corral her brother and her friend. She appeared to shift between irritation and amusement, which was the customary response to Vera and Frederick's shenanigans.

"And you, Freddie dear, should know better. Vera needs our support now, and that's what we're going to give her. Well, that and our sternest, most judgmental review of Jennie Bryer's performance. Do you think you can handle that? Or shall we leave you at home?"

Frederick pursed his lips and turned to approach the bar cart, muttering something about how he hadn't wanted to attend the theater tonight anyway.

Ignoring her brother, Rosemary focused on Vera, who looked, in her opinion, far more like a fairy princess than Rosemary ever would. "I simply cannot believe the director passed you over for the part of Titania. You look perfect for the role just as you are. No costume needed."

Vera's frock, in palest pink, had a shirred shoulder that skimmed down into a fitted, corset-like bodice, then dropped gently to swirl around shapely calves. Sparkling beads sprinkled across the skirt caught the light like tiny, pinprick stars.

"Thank you, Rosie. You always know what to say." Vera kissed Rosemary on the cheek with a genuine smile on her face. "I thought for sure I had that role in the bag. Perhaps I'm not cut out to be an actress, after all." A sliver of doubt crept into her tone.

The mere thought that Vera would think she was less talented than Rosemary knew she was irked, and she shot her friend a scathing glance. "Stop talking like that. You're the daughter of the great Lorraine Blackburn. You have the pedigree, you have the talent, and you—usually—have the ego to match. I much prefer the Vera who knows the director was a dolt to the uncertain woman standing before me. Now, shall we go and discover how badly he got it wrong, or would you rather mope around here and give Jennie the satisfaction of knowing she bested you twice?"

Vera's eyes narrowed, but her spine straightened, and she tilted her nose in the air. "Come on then. We wouldn't want to miss the opening curtain." She strode out of the room followed by Rosemary with Frederick and Desmond on their heels.

CHAPTER FIVE

When they pulled up in front of The Globe, Rosemary was dismayed to see that a line ran out the theater doors and down the block. Her heart sank at the thought of standing on the footway in a pair of new, unbroken-in high heels for the length of time it would take to gain admittance. She scratched an itch on her neck and scowled when she felt the clasp of her necklace catch on her sleeve and break. Into her handbag, it went with a sigh, and she wondered if the night wasn't just set to be a disaster.

"I'm not going to be able to walk tomorrow, Vera," she whined.

Frederick snorted. "Old Des here will have to carry you," he said out of the corner of his mouth and earned himself a sharp elbow to the ribs. "Ouch, Rosie, I was only joking."

"Stop your bickering, children," Vera retorted. "Just because I didn't get picked to play the role of Titania doesn't mean I don't still have friends in high places. Or, at least, friends with access to the side entrance."

Vera instructed Wadsworth where to turn. "Pull up

just there, if you don't mind."

The four piled out of the car and onto the footway, where Vera led them into a short alley and knocked on a door hidden in a shallow alcove. It swung open, and a short, balding man with rosy cheeks peeked out from inside.

"'Ello, Vera. You're looking splendid tonight. Come, come." He motioned them inside and led them along the edge of the backstage area where actors and crew bustled about getting ready for the show. The mixture of excitement, nervousness, and impatience made for an intense atmosphere.

"Hurry up with the corset; I've got to be strapped into this thing by curtain call," one of the actresses snapped at her aide. "I can't imagine how women used to dress this way every day. It's positively barbaric." Rosemary heartily agreed with the sentiment.

"Yes, but they do make for the most amazing view," Frederick snickered to Desmond, who grinned in agreement.

"Shush, Freddie," Rosemary warned, "at least until we get to our seats, and then you can mutter inappropriate remarks under your breath where Vera and I don't have to hear them."

Not in the least bit chagrined, Frederick shut his mouth and made a mental list of inappropriate remarks with which to regale his sister later.

An irritated-looking man shoved past Rosemary on his way towards the back of the stage. He bumped her elbow and sent her handbag flying without a backwards glance, the contents spewing out onto the floor. "Oh no!" she cried, kneeling to retrieve the items from beneath racks of costumes and stacks of stage props.

"Hey there!" Desmond shouted as he took a few steps after the man. "You owe the lady an apology."

The man didn't turn and simply tossed a "bugger off" over his shoulder.

Vera placed a hand on Desmond's arm. "That was the director. Let him be. He seems to be having a fabulously rough go of it," she said cheerily. "Come, our seats are this way."

She thanked the man who had let them through the side entrance, and he winked at her as he circled back in the opposite direction.

Having skipped the queue out the front, the section of ground-level seats where Rosemary and company were situated was relatively empty, and they were allowed an opportunity to watch as the space around them filled with men in their natty suits and women decked out in their best finery.

"Explain to me why we're sitting down here in the stalls," Frederick griped to Vera. "I thought you had more pull than this."

"It's opening night, Freddie," Vera retorted. "All the box seats were sold ages ago. And besides, I happen to think these *are* the best seats in the house. I like to be able to see the nuances of the actors' expressions. Now, why don't you shut up and order a drink so I can tolerate you?"

Frederick obliged, taking Desmond along with him and allowing Rosemary and Vera some moments to people watch. As the sounds of shuffling feet, rustling dresses, and polite conversation rose to a dull roar, Vera fell into an increasingly and uncharacteristically morose silence.

Until that was, she flipped open the playbill and scanned through the section listing the accomplishments of the major players.

"Did you read this … this scandalous horror?" Vera flapped the pamphlet in Rosemary's face. "It's fiction, I tell you. Pure fiction. It lists Jennie Bryer as a former student of both the Royal Academy and The Guildhall School. Look at the dates. Impossible. You know I attended the Royal Academy during the same period, and I can tell you she was not a student while I was there."

The Vera who normally took life with a wink and a smile had flown, leaving this unsettling creature in her place. Rosemary tried to talk her friend around.

"Someone made an error. Maybe the printers mixed her up with someone else."

"More likely she's a scheming, cheating—"

"Excuse us, please." A man's voice interrupted the conversation, and as Rosemary shifted to allow for his passage, she looked up into the eyes of her neighbor Abigail Redberry.

"Oh, hello." Rosemary ignored the seething Vera and said pleasantly, "You look lovely this evening, Abigail." She merely nodded towards the dress Abigail wore, a silvery sheath of beaded silk, but Martin Redberry took notice.

He smiled at his wife indulgently, and Rosemary remembered Abigail's description of teenagers in love. "She absolutely does. Worth every penny, darling." He kissed Abigail full on the lips, bringing a soft smile to the woman's face that made Rosemary's heart ache.

"I should have realized it was this play to which you referred earlier, but I'm happy for the coincidence nonetheless." Rosemary gave Vera a nudge with her elbow.

"My friend, Vera here, was up for the part of Titania. We're tasked with deciding whether the director made the right choice or not." She introduced Vera to Mr. and Mrs. Redberry, who both promised to assess Jennie Bryer's performance with the shrewdest of eyes.

"You're Vera Blackburn!" Abigail's eyes widened with shock and pleasure. "I saw you in a performance of *Othello*, the one in the park a year or so back. I'm a fan!" She looked positively thrilled, and Vera preened at the compliment.

"Thank you so much," Vera replied. "But I don't think the director felt the same way, considering I'm here in the audience instead of backstage waiting for my cue."

Frederick and Desmond chose that moment to return, and a second round of introductions finished up just as the lights blinked to warn that the play would begin shortly.

"Now that I know you might have played Titania, I fear some of the shine has gone from the evening," Abigail assured Vera while her husband nodded in agreement. "However, I will relish your company almost enough to make up for the lack."

Leaning over to talk past Martin, Abigail said, "Darling, didn't I tell you these seats would be the berries?"

In answer, he glanced back and up towards the box seats. "I suppose."

Abigail's cheer could not be contained. "Martin prefers sitting in the back," she explained, "but I always try to get closer to the action. He's a darling to indulge me. I haven't missed a show here for the last three seasons, and box seats are awfully dear."

Vera winked at her. "Well, now I know whom to invite. You'll be better company than this lot, save Rosie here."

Tired of being the man in the middle, Martin suggested a swap so that Abigail could sit on Rosemary's other side during the show. Rosemary watched the couple carefully to see if Martin might exhibit signs of loutish behavior, but it seemed the moment of upset had been forgotten as the man played the attentive husband.

Smiling as if besotted, Martin held Abigail's hand gently in his own; he whispered in her ear, words that turned her lips up into a smile. Still, Rosemary wondered what could have caused a man who appeared so attentive to engage in a screaming match just that morning.

She thought perhaps she'd been hasty to jump to the conclusion that the man was a cad. Anyone could have a beastly day. She wondered why she cared so much anyway; it was absolutely none of her business. She vowed to mind her manners in the future and clasped Vera's hand as the opening curtain rose to reveal a representation of ancient Athens.

As soon as Theseus began lamenting the interminable length of four more days, Rosemary forgot about everything else around her. She enjoyed the rhythm of Shakespeare's cadence, and the complexity of the language, not to mention the elaborate costumes and sets that transported one to a fairy woodland.

Vera's fists clenched and her body went stiff in the seat when Jennie Bryer emerged from between two enormous papier-mâché flowers. She smiled benevolently at the sprites who fluttered around her skirts, anxious to do the queen's bidding.

"Well, she does look the part," Desmond offered in a low voice. "Statuesque with queen-like attributes."

Vera might have let the comment pass as it hadn't been uttered in any leering sort of way, but Frederick spoke up and doomed the pair of them to her bad graces.

"Yes, and just look at those attributes." He earned a pinch for his efforts.

From the corner of her eye, Rosemary watched Vera mouth the words along with Titania. "Met we on hill, in dale, forest, or mead, By pavèd fountain, or by rushy brook, Or in the beachèd margent of the sea—" Jennie Bryer stumbled over the line, and for a moment, her mouth opened and closed without any sound escaping at all.

Vera didn't even try to hide her triumphant smile, but she never said another word during the rest of the performance.

CHAPTER SIX

When the curtain rose for the final time the crowd took to its feet, but in the absence of a second gaffe big enough for a true celebration of Jennie Bryer bungling the part, Vera only allowed herself a half-hearted attempt at applause.

"You would have performed the role brilliantly, Vera," Rosemary assured her friend.

"Jennie did a credible job, but I wouldn't call it a spectacular performance, to be sure," Abigail contributed with enough sincerity that Rosemary decided she liked the woman even more.

"Thank you for saying so," Vera replied. "Would you and your husband like to accompany us backstage? My friend Samuel played the part of Bottom, and I'd like to tell him what a splendid job he did."

Abigail looked at Martin, her eyes sparkling, "Oh, can we, please?"

"Of course, my love," Martin agreed. "Your wish is my command. I do demand we retire for drinks afterward, as I wouldn't mind washing the excess of Shakespearean prose from my memory."

Frederick craned his neck around Vera and Rosemary to heartily agree. "Desmond and I concur. In fact, why don't we get a table at that pub just around the corner, and you can meet us there when you've finished?"

Rosemary thought Frederick's idea an excellent one. Even if Jennie hadn't bungled Titania to Vera's satisfaction, there was no denying the woman had looked magnificent onstage. It would be best if he and Desmond resurrected their discussion of her finer attributes well out of Vera's earshot. Not, of course, that Desmond would purposely utter a word intended to infuriate Vera—he knew better than to poke a raging lioness. Besides, he'd been too busy surreptitiously watching Rosemary's facial expressions during every scene to ogle Jennie anyway.

With a plan in place to spend a scant few minutes congratulating Vera's friend before catching up with Frederick and Desmond, the Redberrys followed Vera and Rosemary to the backstage area where the latter had arrived at the start of the night.

Before the show, the atmosphere had been hopeful, but now it fluctuated between frustration and elation; those who felt they had played their parts well exhibiting the latter, while the actors who had missed a line or a cue displaying the former.

"This is so exciting!" Abigail whistled out a breath and clutched her husband's hand. "I've never been backstage before." Wide eyes took in the whole beehive of activity behind the scenes: actors wearing various bits and pieces of costume, stagehands tearing down and setting up for the next run, props being gathered and returned to their places.

They found Vera's friend easily enough, as he was sitting in front of a mirror and wiping the last of the donkey makeup off his face. After planting a kiss on his cheek, Vera gushed over his hilarious portrayal of an overzealous actor who found himself entangled and then dragged into the middle of an argument between the faerie king and queen.

"You were simply marvelous, darling Samuel," Vera concluded sincerely. "If I weren't leaving for a holiday tomorrow afternoon, I would make a point of attending the entire run of shows if only to cheer you on."

"You are too kind, and you know it, Vera dear," Samuel replied. "You must have caught my stumble in the second act, and I felt as though my Bottom could have been a bit more whimsical."

"Perhaps if you'd been cast alongside an actress worth her salt, you'd have had more to play off," Vera said wryly, and then took a surreptitious look around for Jennie Bryer.

Unfortunately for her, the actress in question had been seated at a mirror on the opposite side of Samuel's, and when she poked her head around the corner to see who'd had the temerity to critique her performance, her eyes narrowed into dangerous slits.

"What are you doing back here, Vera Blackburn? This area is for members of the company only, and the last time I checked, you were not included in that group." There was such derision in her tone as to send blood rushing into Rosemary's cheeks, abruptly turning them to flags of red, and she automatically opened her mouth to defend her friend.

She needn't have worried, because Vera was more

than capable of taking care of herself. Before Rosemary could get a breath out, Vera pierced Jennie with a look and retorted, "And what exactly did you have to do to get the part, Jennie? Take a little after-hours romp with the esteemed director? At least I have enough pride not to stoop that low."

The most poisonous of snakes couldn't have held more venom than the smile Vera turned towards her nemesis.

Rosemary glanced between the two women as animosity built until the pressure nearly made her ears pop. Abigail clutched her husband's arm, her breath hitching, and her eyes sparkling with excitement. The scene playing out before them was better than anything they'd witnessed on the stage that evening.

"Your pride isn't worth nearly as much as your mother's money, is it? How lovely for you not to have to worry about paying the bills. Acting isn't a flight of fancy for the rest of us as it is for you. It's not all fun and games. When you've finished for the evening, you get to cool your heels in a lavish flat while the rest of us work for a living. You don't have the drive or the hunger to succeed, and you never will. You'll end up a no-name has-been, just like your mother, mark my words!"

Jennie Bryer had gone too far. The next moments seemed to crawl past, and still, Rosemary couldn't have warned Jennie in time to duck. Nor would she have, since she considered the punishment far less than the crime deserved.

Light glinted off her diamond ring as Vera reared back and curled her hand into a fist. She might have stopped herself, even hesitated for a fraction of a second, but Jennie smirked, and that was all it took to push her over the edge.

Arrowing towards its target, Vera's fist landed with a dull thud that sent Jennie reeling back a few steps. Scarlet erupted from her lip, and her eyes widened as she touched the painful spot and came back with bloodstained fingertips. Abigail, upon seeing the spout of blood, grimaced and turned away.

"How dare you!" Jennie cried, whirling towards the mirror to examine her face. "You could have knocked my teeth out, you jealous, horrible witch!" Two strides had her standing eye to eye with Vera, whose face had contorted into an expression displaying both satisfaction and shame.

Jennie hauled back as if to return the blow, but Samuel grabbed her and pinned her arms behind her back. "Let go of me!" she screeched, drawing the attention of everyone within hearing distance, which included the entire company and the director.

"Let me take a look," Martin said in the tone adults usually reserve for small children or yapping dogs. "I'm a dentist."

The girl allowed Martin to examine her, and Rosemary noted that he was extremely gentle for a dentist. "You're going to be just fine. Ice that lip, but your teeth are intact." He pulled a business card out of his pocket and deposited it in Jennie's clean hand. "Call me if you experience pain or if you feel any shifting of the teeth."

"I think it's time for us to go, Vera," Rosemary said, shooting an apologetic glance at Abigail and Martin and pulling Vera towards the door.

"You're banned from all further performances, Miss Blackburn," the director informed her in an icy tone as they passed him on their way out. Head bowed, Vera nodded and made a hasty retreat along with the rest of the group.

Once outside, Vera crumpled and apologized. "I'm sorry you had to see that." She directed the sentiment towards Abigail and Martin since Rosemary was already well acquainted with her temper.

"Oh, don't apologize! The events of this evening were most exciting. Believe me, aside from the blood, I'm having an absolutely fabulous time!" Abigail gushed. Martin smiled tightly and nodded absently in agreement, his gaze having settled upon something across the street.

When he spoke, his voice sounded choked. "You three go on ahead. I'll meet you at the pub in a few minutes. I have some business to attend to." With that, he dropped his wife's hand and walked off in the opposite direction.

"Martin!" Abigail called to her husband's retreating back. "Of all the nerve." She turned to Rosemary, her face flushed. "I've been abandoned like something meant for the bin. Oh, I could simply kill him for the way he's been acting lately."

If there was one thing Vera could never resist, it was the urge to cheer up the downtrodden. "Come now," she said, slinging an arm over Abigail's shoulder. "No use letting that flat tire spoil your mood. Let's get—what was the term Freddie used? Spifflicated."

As willing as a puppy, Abigail followed Vera towards the pub.

Rosemary's curiosity got the best of her, and she craned her neck to see what it was that had caused

Martin to abandon his wife on the street. He was talking to a tall, thickly muscled man, and though his back was turned so that she couldn't see his face, Martin appeared more than annoyed. He gesticulated wildly for a moment but kept his voice low enough that from that distance, Rosemary couldn't hear what he was saying.

Feeling like a voyeur, Rosemary returned her attention to Vera and Abigail, who were laughing heartily by the time the trio reached the pub across the street.

"You mean we missed all the excitement, *and* the opportunity to see Jennie Bryer undressing?" Frederick whined once the tale had been retold to his satisfaction a solid three times.

Martin, who'd joined them just a couple of moments after they'd ordered drinks, brightened infinitesimally. "It was a sight to see, I'll vouch for that."

"Vera was fantastic," Rosemary enthused. "It's a wonder she didn't break the poor girl's nose."

"*Poor girl*," Vera harrumphed. "Considering what she said to me, that *poor girl* is lucky I didn't do more than tussle with her." Her voice had begun to slur thanks in large part to the second G&T an enthusiastic Frederick had just lavished upon her.

"She might have a point, Vera darling," he said, winking in Desmond's direction. His friend, at least, had the sense to keep his mouth firmly shut other than to offer congratulations to Vera. True, Desmond had spent countless hours with the group as a child, but it had been years since then, and he judged wisely that he ought to get the lay of the land before invoking Vera's wrath.

What he remembered of her was that she'd been a

spunky, fearless girl who'd played as roughly as any of the boys. In fact, sometimes even more so in an attempt to prove herself just as tough. It appeared she hadn't changed much, and if pressed, he would admit he admired her tenacity. As far as Rosemary went, there were plenty of attributes to admire there, but he was wise enough to keep his thoughts on those to himself, as well.

"What do you mean, she might have a point?" Vera demanded, the color rising in her cheeks. Rosemary pushed herself away from the table slightly, just in case Vera came to blows again. She didn't want to get caught in the crossfire.

Frederick gulped, realizing he might have bitten off a bit more than he could chew, but refused to backtrack. This was how their arguments always started: Frederick poking at Vera and Vera shoving back at him. "Well, you aren't counting on a paycheck, are you? She's not wrong about that. Perhaps a degree of financial insecurity provides a higher level of motivation." He sat back, eyes twinkling, and waited for the onslaught.

Vera, angry but also well on her way to being completely ossified, raised an eyebrow while contemplating how to respond.

Martin spoke up in her favor, earning him a few points in her esteem. "In my own experience, you can never tell what might drive a person to do anything."

"Fair point, my friend," Frederick said, nodding to Martin in thanks for taking the heat off him for even a second. "Fair point."

"That is true," Vera slurred, "and we know from firsthand experience, don't we, Rosie?" She tried to wink, but it came off as more of a flutter of the lashes and Rosemary wondered whether she ought to get just as sozzled. Vera, in a combative mood was much easier to take when one was also carrying an edge.

"What is she talking about?" Abigail asked, avid with curiosity about the look that passed between Rosemary and Vera—and even more curious about Vera in general. The way the woman goggled, she might as well have been sitting across from the Queen of England.

Rosemary leaned over the table towards Abigail, but before she could get out so much as a word, Frederick beat her to it.

"Rosie here is the next best thing to Sherlock Holmes. A regular sleuth, don't you know?"

"A private dick they call them in the States," Desmond added to the conversation. "Or would that make her a dickess? One can never be sure about these things."

Deep in his cups, Frederick found the term inordinately amusing. "Whatever you call it, she is the one who solved the murder at Barton Manor. You must have read about it in the papers. Of course, the police took all the credit, but Rosemary and Vera almost got themselves killed tracking down the culprit." His voice rang with pride as if he'd forgotten how terrified he'd been at the time.

"Oh, Freddie, hush," Rosemary admonished. "It wasn't as thrilling as you're making it out to be. We simply put the pieces together, is all."

Vera guffawed. "It certainly was that thrilling, and you know it. I have no problem taking a bit of the credit. We only narrowly escaped death!" She'd become even further intoxicated and, having missed the opportunity to perform onstage, even more theatrical than usual.

She told the tale, and by the end of it, had everyone cheering for herself and Rosemary. Martin peered at Rosemary with newfound respect, and Abigail could barely contain her excitement. His hand rested on her back, and it appeared his transgression from earlier had been entirely forgotten.

When Vera moved on from true life events, she began reciting Titania's lines from *A Midsummer Night's Dream*. Nearby patrons, most of them well greased, egged her on. Before anyone could stop her, Vera had mounted the bar to stand and deliver her lines to the packed house, and despite having consumed a number of cocktails, she never missed a word. The performance would have put Jennie Byers to shame had she walked through the door.

By the time Frederick and Desmond had persuaded Vera from her perch atop the bar, Martin had reached his limit, "I have early patients in the morning, dear. Are you ready?" He yawned, and Abigail reluctantly agreed it was time to depart for home.

"I'll see you all soon, I hope," she said as she made her way to the exit after an enthusiastic hug and a kiss from Vera that was meant for Abigail's cheek but landed somewhere near her ear instead.

CHAPTER SEVEN

Sometime during the early hours of the morning—or, at least, what seemed the early hours but was coming on for noon—Rosemary awoke with a hammer in her head and her stomach tied in knots. Silently, she cursed her friends for pressing too many cocktails into her hand the night before. She moaned and tried with little success to wrench the covers free from Vera's grip.

The ringing in her ears gave way to the shrill tones of a whistle, and for a moment, Rosemary thought her head might fall off. Immediately following came the thought that losing her head might not be a bad thing. Vera stirred, shoved the sleep mask off her eyes, and turned towards Rosemary with an equally confused expression on her face. "What on earth is that noise?" she asked sleepily.

"Police whistle. More than one, I think. Or we're having a simultaneous auditory hallucination," Rosemary replied, peeling herself off the bed and crossing to the window that looked out over her front doorstep. "Probably an accident around the corner. I can't see from here." She flopped back down onto the bed and closed her eyes.

"Rosie, come on. We're not going to get back to sleep with this racket, and we have to catch a train in a few hours anyway. Besides, I'm curious, and I know you are, too." Vera jumped off the bed with more vigor than she ought to have had, considering how much she'd had to drink the previous evening.

Rosemary opened her eyes and glared at her friend, but allowed herself to be pulled into a standing position. She dressed quickly, as did Vera, and they headed downstairs. There, they found a disheveled-looking Frederick accompanied by Desmond, who looked fresh as a daisy, peeking through the windows in an attempt to discern the origin of the unrelenting ringing.

"I see I was the only frugal drinker last evening," Desmond commented with a glint in his eye.

"Shut up, Des," Frederick fired back after taking a sip of black coffee with his eyes closed against the pounding in his head.

Rosemary strode towards the front door. "I'm going to go for a short walk around the block. Anyone care to accompany me?" Of course, everyone did, and the foursome trooped out to the footway to investigate the disturbance.

As she rounded the corner, Rosemary's eyes widened at the sight of two police vehicles parked in front of Dr. Redberry's office entrance. She saw Abigail standing near the gate, breathed a sigh of relief, and then put a hand to her head as another whistle blast sounded. Vera and the men, feigning politeness, hung back a short distance away and looked on with concern.

By the look on Abigail's face, something terrible had

happened, and Rosemary's heart leaped into her throat. Before she had a chance to make her inquiry, a constable exited the office and said to the officer still stationed outside, "The medical examiner will be along shortly, along with the inspector."

All Rosemary could think about was how Abigail would survive the loss of her husband. She knew the experience firsthand and had nearly lost herself when Andrew passed away. The horror of it came crashing back, and she instinctively reached out to take Abigail's hand, her face filled with empathy for the woman. "Oh, Abigail," she cried.

"It's not Martin," Abigail said, having watched the cycle of emotions and understanding the conclusion to which Rosemary had jumped. "It's one of his patients. They're interviewing Martin now. Do you think we should call our solicitor?"

Abigail looked past Rosemary to Vera and the men, her eyes wide with worry. Her hands were shaking, but otherwise, she appeared steady. Rosemary judged that Abigail was running on adrenaline, given the circumstances, and would eventually and inevitably crash once the excitement had died down.

"I think," Rosemary said slowly, "it would be best to let events play out until a determination is made. Do they seem to think the circumstances around the death are suspicious? What happened, exactly?"

Abigail sighed. "He died in the chair. They suspect from an overdose of nitrous oxide." She looked around and lowered her voice. "Martin mentioned they were having problems with the valves, and that he had to take precautions to ensure the dosage was correct. I think they're considering it an accident at this point; however, mightn't it be prudent to hedge our bets?"

"Perhaps," Rosemary agreed, choosing her next words carefully, "though in my experience, calling for a solicitor too early tends to make one look guilty in the eyes of the police. For now, I would advise waiting for a beat to see how things develop. Speak to Martin, and then make that decision together."

"Thank you for the advice, Rosemary," Abigail said sincerely. "It must be comforting in times like these to have experience in such matters."

Rosemary smiled tightly. "Yes, in a way it is, I suppose." She fetched her friends, and at Abigail's request, invited them to stand and wait until Martin had finished giving his statement.

When Maximilian Whittington pulled up in front of Dr. Redberry's office, he was both irritated and secretly pleased that he recognized three out of the five people draped over the fence. If his heart settled into an uneven rhythm, it was only because he feared he might once again find himself having to defend Frederick Woolridge's innocence—it had nothing whatsoever to do with how beautiful Rosemary looked in her summer dress, her face flushed with the heat of the sun.

He'd been close friends with her husband, Andrew Lillywhite, since their days on the police force, before Andrew had fallen in love and decided he preferred private investigation to traditional police work. Max had known Andrew better than almost anyone; he'd respected him, and that meant that he had no intention of acting upon the flood of longing he felt when he recognized Rosemary's golden hair.

Or when her face lit up the moment she caught sight of him. "Max! Oh, thank goodness you're here. Abigail, you're in good hands, dear. Inspector Whittington is the best we have. He'll make sure to take good care of Martin, won't you, Max?" Her eyelashes fluttered, and whether her intent had been to dazzle him or not, he found himself nodding in agreement.

"I take it you are the wife of Dr. Redberry?" he asked, tearing his eyes away from Rosemary's face with an effort.

Abigail nervously dipped her head. "Yes, I'm Abigail Redberry. Pleased to meet you."

"And you," Max replied. "Now, please excuse me while I consult with my constables. I'll return to ask for your statement when I've finished speaking to your husband."

"Of course, of course. You must do your job. Please excuse me; this has come as quite a shock. Martin is good at his work. We don't usually have dead men in the house. As you can imagine, it's quite unnerving." Abigail wrung her hands, and her eyes widened until she looked stunned with shock yet again.

"We'll stay here with you, won't we?" Rosemary directed the last towards her friends, who were all as interested in the outcome as she was.

"Why don't we go around the corner and take a rest on your front doorstep, Abigail?" she asked as the medical examiner's vehicle arrived. The last thing Abigail needed to see was the body being carted out of the house. Gently, Rosemary guided her neighbor around the corner and out of sight of the more grisly details.

On their way past the lower-level window that allowed a bit of light into Martin's office, Rosemary kicked a few stray cigarette butts out of the way and made a mental note to ask Helen to do the Redberrys a favor and sweep the footway free of debris. It irked her that people cared so little about the aesthetics of the neighborhood, but there wasn't time to stew about that while she carried on down the block.

CHAPTER EIGHT

When Max had concluded his questioning almost an hour later and pulled Abigail aside to speak to her privately, Rosemary had a chance to confer with her friends.

"We've two hours left before we catch the train. Is there a way to get out of this situation with any sort of sympathy?" Frederick asked, for once having left his sarcasm at home.

Rosemary sighed. "I don't know. It feels wrong to leave without knowing the possible outcome. I should like to speak to Max first to see what his thoughts are on the death. I don't know why, but I feel an obligation to Abigail. She's been going through a rough time, and I get the sense she doesn't have many people other than Martin to lean on in times of trouble."

"It's perfectly fine, Rosie," Vera reassured her. "We'll take a later train if we must." She shot a scathing look at Frederick as if challenging him to contest the decision. "It's not as though any of us are on a time constraint, what with my lack of an acting job and Frederick's sabbatical."

At that, Frederick returned Vera's glare. It wasn't something he wanted to think about, much less talk about. Having been forced to take a break from his family's business after also being accused of murder was a sore spot, to say the least.

Desmond, seeing the expression on Frederick's face, spoke up. "I'm free as a bird as well. I'd say a death next door qualifies as good enough reason to postpone for a day. I'm intrigued, and what's more, I like the Redberrys. I think we'll all feel better knowing this matter is settled before we go off on holiday."

"Okay, then, it's decided. I'll run and let Wadsworth know," Vera offered, skipping up the steps to Rosemary's house and disappearing through the front door.

"Rosemary, may I speak with you?" Max broke away from the Redberrys.

"Is there anything you can tell me?" she asked without preamble.

Max ran a hand through his hair. "There isn't much to tell yet. It appears to have been an unfortunate accident. We'll investigate, of course, but there's no reason for you to worry, as I'm certain the evidence will bear out my initial findings. There's no need for you to hone your investigative skills. This was an accidental death."

Despite the gravity of the situation, Rosemary allowed herself the tiniest of smiles. "Max, if I didn't know better, I'd say you were warning me off your territory."

"You may take my caution as such, but I only meant to reassure you. Did I overhear you saying you were going on holiday?" he asked, glancing towards Desmond, who stood next to Frederick and watched the conversation between Max and Rosemary with avid interest.

"Yes, that was the plan," Rosemary explained. "Vera and I decided some sun and sand were in order. When Frederick heard, he decided to horn in and to bring along his old school chum Desmond to round out the numbers. We were supposed to leave on the four o'clock train, but we've opted to wait a day or two in light of what's happened."

After a pause, Max said, "I see no reason you should postpone your holiday." It cost him something to encourage her to run off to spend time on the beach with a handsome man.

"Aren't you going to also warn me to keep my pretty little nose out of other people's business?" Rosemary asked with a smirk. "It makes no difference; Abigail is a new friend, and I won't relax until I know her husband isn't being put up on charges."

The inspector had attempted to discourage Rosemary's involvement with another untimely death, and felt he'd done his duty to the best of his ability. He didn't know why he'd even bothered to try to talk any sense into her anyway; Rosemary would do precisely as she pleased. What was more, she would act as though it were entirely reasonable for her to do so.

Halfway through the conversation, he'd realized he'd engaged in an exercise in futility, and that he might as well accept her position.

Max sighed. "Is there really any point in arguing? I'm not sure why I bother. There's nothing to indicate foul play, but you won't be satisfied until you see for yourself."

Max noted the determined set of Rosemary's shoulders and assumed the flare of satisfaction he felt was down to the fact she wouldn't be investigating another murder. It had nothing at all to do about postponing a trip with another man in tow.

"I give up, Rosemary. Do whatever it is you feel you must. Where were you headed, anyway?"

"Cyprus. Have you ever been?"

"No, no, I haven't," Max said, but he sounded as though he'd barely registered Rosemary's question.

Concern tugged at Rosemary until she frowned up at him. "What's going on with you, Max?" Now that she had taken a closer look, he appeared drawn and slightly haggard, a state she'd never seen him in before. She didn't like it. She preferred Max looking as he always did: confident and in control.

They had wandered away from the group during the course of the conversation. Now, Max took a seat on a conveniently placed park bench and indicated for Rosemary to join him. "I have a lot on my mind. I don't want to trouble you, but it would help to talk about it if you're willing to listen."

"Of course, Max. Tell me what's bothering you." It was nice to speak to someone who didn't treat her like she already had all the problems she could possibly handle—and it was equally nice to engage in a conversation with a man who didn't seem to consider vulnerability a weakness. Most of them preferred to keep their problems to themselves for fear of appearing weak, but Max wasn't like most men.

"I'm up for a promotion," he said.

"Why, that's wonderful news." One would think such

an honor would put a smile on a man's face.

Max went on to explain. "The promotion would mean a transfer to another unit. One a good distance outside of London."

Now it was Rosemary's turn to feel a pang of worry. "Oh, I see."

"My superiors want me to take the position, and I might, eventually, be able to return to the city. However, the opportunity is poorly timed. You see, my mother is ailing, and since my father died, she's been caring for the house and gardens all alone."

When Rosemary merely blinked, Max pinched the bridge of his nose and asked, "Did I never tell you about my misspent youth?"

"Knowing you as I do now," Rosemary smiled, "I can hardly picture you as a young rogue bent on terrorizing the countryside."

Max gave a low chuckle and capitulated. "An exaggeration on my part. I was born here in London, but my parents relocated while I was still in my pram. Father purchased a house in the country along with an aging nursery, and with my mother's assistance, restored its fortunes. Both my parents were passionate gardeners. Sadly, their talent with growing things did not pass along to me, nor did any interest in taking over the family business."

Fascinated, Rosemary listened intently.

"I still enjoy visiting, but I prefer the pace of city life. Perhaps if I ever have a wife and children, we'll buy a summer home someplace where there are more trees than buildings." Max's eyes took on a dreamy look, and he had to shake his head to dislodge an image that he would never be able to share with Rosemary. It featured her in a field of rolling hills, a paintbrush in her hand, and a passel of children at her skirts.

"The house and gardens are far too much for Mother to handle these days. Furthermore, she's gone through every available gardener in the area. Ariadne Whittington has her own way of doing things, and she doesn't appreciate opposing opinions."

In a dry tone, Rosemary pointed out, "It seems you and your mother have many things in common even if horticulture isn't one of them."

Max let the subtle criticism slide by without comment. "She has a generous offer for the property, so there's no reason for her to stay on in the house alone. Except, of course, that she doesn't want to leave and is determined to detest cottage I've picked out for her. Admittedly, it needs quite a bit of work doing, and definitely a woman's touch. I thought perhaps, that if she was able to decorate it herself, she might find a way to make it feel more like home, but she's taken little interest in the task. In fact, she refuses to put so much as a toe over the threshold."

Rosemary thought about her parents and their house out in Pardington. Evelyn Woolridge wouldn't deign to tend her own gardens, of course—she had staff for that—but Rosemary could only imagine what sort of fit her mother would throw if it were suggested she ought to move to the city. Then she thought about Max moving *out* of the city, and that plan didn't appeal to her either. She liked knowing he was nearby, even if she hadn't reached out as often as she—as often as either of them—would have liked.

"What can I do to help?"

"I was wondering if you might like to look at the cottage and give me a woman's perspective on how to make it more appealing."

"Well, you've come to the right person. You remember what this place looked like when we moved in." Rosemary gestured towards her townhouse. "It was practically in a shambles and had the ugliest decor imaginable. It appears I've got an extra day or so. I'd be happy to come for a visit and give you my thoughts," she offered.

Max let out an enormous sigh, and Rosemary thought she noticed the shadow of a smile lift the corners of his mouth. "I would appreciate that, Rosemary, but only if you're sure you have the time," he said, thinking how lovely it would be to spend some time alone with her.

"It's the least I can do. After all, you did save my life, Max." Rosemary smiled, and his heart skipped another beat. "When you're finished here, come back for me. I'm sure my brother and Vera can find some way to entertain themselves and Desmond for a few hours."

Once the medical examiner had finished his job, and Max had adequately questioned everybody present at the time of death, the dentist was finally allowed to return to the home above his office. If he felt any annoyance at the sight of guests at the dining room table, he didn't let it show.

Abigail had insisted upon inviting Rosemary and her friends in for tea, and though she appeared merely to have been acting in a neighborly fashion, Rosemary shrewdly suspected there was more to it than that. The woman needed support, and that was exactly what she would get. It didn't matter to Rosemary that they hadn't been the closest of friends up until now. There was something she liked about Abigail, and she found she wanted to help her if it was within her power to do so.

"Thank you for staying with my wife," Martin said to the group. "This was no time for her to be left alone, but I do hope we haven't kept you from anything."

"Nothing of import," Rosemary replied easily, her friends nodding in agreement. "We're sorry for what happened, Martin. I know the death was an accident, but I'm sure it weighs heavily on you." She could tell it did: his eyes were rimmed with red, and his shoulders slumped.

"Yes, it certainly is. I pride myself on ensuring my patients' safety, and today, I failed in that effort. At the cost of a man's life." He sat down on one of the chairs and rested his elbows on the table. Abigail went to him and placed a comforting hand on his shoulder.

"I'm sure I shut off the gas when I left the examination room. I'm sure of it," Martin kept repeating as if saying it over and over might make it true. "Poor old Mrs. Linley. I do hope the ordeal didn't traumatize her overmuch."

"I'm sure Mrs. Linley is just fine, Martin," Abigail assured him. "When you're going on eighty years of age, the chances are you've seen a dead body or two." She grimaced and sat back in her chair with a sigh.

Feeling as though their welcome was wearing thin, Rosemary stood and indicated that she and her friends would be on their way. "I'm sure the two of you have much to discuss."

"If you need anything at all, we shall be right next door," Vera contributed, casting a sympathetic look in Abigail's direction. Desmond and Frederick, who had been uncharacteristically quiet, shook Martin's hand. The dentist appeared dazed but accepted the gesture with an appreciative grimace.

"Thank you all," Martin said simply and allowed the group to file out of the dining room door.

CHAPTER NINE

"What did I tell you, Des? Spend some time with Rosie here, and undoubtedly, a dead body will turn up," Frederick joked while he passed around cocktails to take the edge off the day. How he could have recovered so quickly from his hangover was beyond Rosemary's comprehension, but she did believe a little hair of the dog might be just what the doctor ordered.

With a narrow-eyed glare at her brother, she qualified, "It's only the second time this has happened, Frederick, and you know it. Besides, in this instance, the death was an accident."

"You don't honestly believe that, do you?" Frederick asked with a smirk, to which Rosemary simply grimaced.

Vera answered instead. "We don't know anything yet, but there's definitely something off about the good Dr. Redberry. Did anyone else notice how his mood swung back and forth like a pendulum all last night? Poor Abigail, having to deal with that type of temperament all the time. That, my friends, is why I think I've decided marriage might not be for me."

Frederick snorted. "Has it ever been?"

"There was a time when I thought, perhaps, if the right man came along," Vera mused. "It's become increasingly obvious that he simply doesn't exist. I'd kill myself if I ever ended up in a marriage like Abigail's and Martin's."

Under his breath, Frederick muttered something about Vera being unable to find anyone willing to deal with her for the rest of his life.

"You know she could cover all ten fingers and toes with the engagement rings she's been offered, brother dear," Rosemary admonished him.

"Fools and saps, fools and saps," Frederick mused with a smile.

Vera merely raked him up and down with an icy look that implied he wasn't man enough to handle her anyway. In return, her tossed her an insouciant grin while Rosemary and Desmond shared a look of amusement.

"You know," Desmond said, throwing fuel on the fire, "I've often wondered if these childish exchanges are merely a cover for some raging attraction you two refuse to acknowledge." Raising his glass, he gave a silent toast to Vera and Frederick. "Seems to me you ought to indulge in a good bout of snogging and get it over with one way or the other."

Rosemary let out an unladylike snort. She'd long harbored similar thoughts, but out of concern for her own skin had kept them to herself. Still, she warned Desmond. "Be careful, Des. Vera has plenty of bite to go with her bark."

"What does that make me? A harmless puppy?"

Frederick retorted.

Surprisingly, Vera came to his defense. "You are a tiger, my darling. Nothing less."

Since none of them could be certain whether the comment was a compliment or an insult, Desmond opted to change the subject back to Abigail and Martin.

"Abigail seems like a good egg, but I don't think we ought to pin all their troubles on poor Dr. Redberry. There are always two sides to any story, and the truth usually lies somewhere in between. She's stronger than she lets on, mark my words."

"Maybe so," Rosemary replied. "Today's tragedy will surely test the mettle of their marriage."

"Speaking of testing one's mettle, Rosie my love, tell me your cook isn't making her famous game pie." Frederick's face went positively green at the thought.

"What's wrong with game pie?" Desmond wanted to know. "I quite like a good game pie."

"Ah," Frederick said, wagging a finger. "There's the rub, you see. Good game pie isn't as heavy as an iron doorstop."

Vera couldn't resist adding, "With nearly the same flavor."

"Whatever cook ends up serving, you will have to eat it or not without me, for I have a dinner engagement with Max. I've agreed to have a look around and see if the flat he's purchased for his ailing mother can be made more enticing."

"Here now, that sounds like a deuced lot of work to do for someone who's merely an acquaintance."

Desmond's outburst tickled Vera enough to have her smiling behind her hand, but Rosemary took it at face value.

"Max is a dear friend, you know. I'm happy to lend him my expertise."

Leaving the room, Rosemary missed Desmond's scowl.

"Hello, Rosemary. Are you ready?" Max asked upon Wadsworth ushering him into the parlor. He looked around, wondering to what remote corner the rest of her entourage had disappeared—particularly, the good-looking man he'd seen eying Rosemary earlier in the day. Loathe to pry, he refrained from asking and found himself relieved not to have to contend with anyone else for her attention.

As Vera, Frederick, and Desmond took themselves off to the dining room, Rosemary had realized that she had never actually been alone with Max in a social capacity. Of course, she had hosted dinners and parties when Andrew was alive, and Max had always been one of the guests she'd gravitated towards, but that had been a different environment altogether.

In fact, being alone with a man who was neither her husband nor her brother was a departure for Rosemary. Her stomach tied itself in knots, and then untied again when she realized that the man in question was merely Max, and therefore, she had no reason to worry.

"Yes, I'm ready," she replied, realizing Max was looking at her expectantly since she had yet to answer his question. "Before we go, have you any news on the case? Poor Abigail, I wouldn't like to leave her in a time of trouble, but we do have a train to catch two days hence if you're quite certain the death was accidental."

"While I commend you for wanting to stand by a friend, you can put your mind at rest. I have no reason to believe the ruling will be anything other than death by misadventure."

He led her to his car, and during the short drive eastward, kept up a running commentary that helped to dissipate the tension Rosemary had been feeling. He declined to discuss further the unfortunate death that had taken place next door, and for that, she was grateful.

"The flat has two bedrooms, a parlor, and a sitting room in addition to the kitchen and dining areas. No servants' quarters, but Mother never was keen on other people living in her house. A housekeeper will come in during the week, but I'm sure that's all she will allow."

As with everything he did, Max drove with great care and competence, his hands sure on the wheel, his eyes scanning the street for possible hazards.

"Mother tends not to get along with kitchen staff. It all comes down to her scandalous preference for vegetables that have not been cooked to mush. Every so often, Father would insist on trying out a new cook. Not one of them lasted a week, and so after a day of tending plants, Mother prepared all our meals." Smiling fondly, he added, "She sang while she worked."

Rosemary listened to Max's ramblings with interest. Most of the conversations they'd had in the past centered around police work or more mundane matters such as the weather or the ever-changing post-war political climate. Imagining him as a child, running around in dirty dungarees planting flowers, made her see him in an entirely different light.

"She sounds lovely. I can't imagine how she must feel

about selling the place and moving to the city."

Max's eyes flashed. "She's positively broken up about it, and I can't even blame her. The house and gardens were her life—hers and Father's—and they both put their hearts and souls into the work. I suppose you can't halt the ravages of time, but it feels an awful lot like the end of an era."

"How do you feel about it?" Rosemary asked, casting a sideways glance towards the driver's seat.

His face went blank for a moment, and then he caught her eye out of the corner of his. "You know, I've been so concerned about Mother, I hadn't thought about myself overmuch. Sad, I suppose." He sighed and paused for a moment. "More than sad, if I'm honest. I offered to move home and run the nursery."

"One can always count on you, Max, to do the right thing, even at great personal cost."

Was she paying him a compliment or not? Max couldn't be certain.

"Do you think me a martyr?"

Rosemary took in his profile and determined by the set of his chin that she'd caused offense.

"Certainly not. Merely conflicted by an impossible choice between a fondly remembered past and the present, which is an absolutely normal reaction. You don't have to want the rural life to mourn the loss of it. It's better you realize it now than discover after six months you miss the city and don't want to trim another rose bush as long as you live. From what you've said, your mother wouldn't want you to give up on something you love just to make her happy—unless I'm mistaken."

"No. You are correct." Max smiled. "She isn't angry

with me, and when I told her I would resign from the force, she threatened to hit me with a garden hoe if I ever brought it up again. She informed me there was an offer on the place just to prove her point."

"It sounds as though she needed a little time to work her way around to the idea of moving. Maybe she'll even learn to like it here if it means spending more time with you."

Max wondered if Rosemary's comment contained a subtle hint about her thoughts on his impending promotion. She had only to ask, to indicate her preference for his continued company, and he'd turn the offer down without a second thought.

"See this park we're passing? The flat is just on the other side of the gardens where she'll have a view of them out of her back windows and the Thames on the other side. Now, if only I can transform the inside to something a bit more to her liking."

Rosemary assured him they would do just that, and suddenly lamented the fact that she would be leaving soon. Helping Max leaped to the top of her priority list, and it disappointed her to know she wouldn't be as involved as she would have liked to be. Also, she had a hankering to meet the mother of this man who cared enough to give up his own life to make the last portion of hers more comfortable.

Little did she know that Max was thinking the very same thing. His mother would absolutely adore Rosemary, and that was saying something since Mrs. Whittington was the most discerning of women. Both were quiet until Max pulled up outside a charming, ivy-covered stone building trimmed with rough-hewn boards that looked to have been installed at least a couple of centuries before.

"It's like a little haven, tucked away down this back street. It feels like we're miles away from the city!" Rosemary exclaimed when she extracted herself from the vehicle and took a good look at Mrs. Whittington's new home.

Max grinned from ear to ear. "Let's hope Mother feels the same way."

Instead of entering through the front, Max led the way to a garden gate inside an arbor overgrown and dripping with ivy. "There is a small plot, barely as large as her kitchen garden back home, but I suspect she'll enjoy a good putter once she's feeling better."

"It's overgrown, but if I squint, I can see how utterly charming it will look when it's put to rights. An oasis of calm. You chose well, Max."

"Wait until you see inside before you rush to judgment." With that, Max tugged on a loose piece of trim that pulled away to reveal a hidden key he used to open the door.

Inside, it appeared the previous tenant had a penchant for dark woodwork and equally dreary wallpaper. Rosemary felt as though she were walking into a cave when she entered the front parlor, but the wood floors only needed a good sanding and a fresh coat of varnish to bring them back to life.

"Imagine if you painted the wainscot a light, airy color and covered the rest with new paper—something flowered, I think, would be best," Rosemary allowed her vision of the room to come to life as she walked through the space, gesturing towards what she would change and what she would keep the same.

"Of course, the woodwork needs refreshing, but you won't want to get rid of the patina altogether. She'll have indoor plants, I imagine—that window seat is lovely, but the window is wide enough that you could build some open shelving up the sides so she can view the river through a frame of leaves and blooms."

Max followed Rosemary's gaze around the room, listening as she explained what she would do. So clearly did she describe her vision that it came to life. He pictured the changes sweeping around the room and turning it into a light, airy space his mother would love. Moving on to the other rooms of the flat, Rosemary kept up her running commentary, even giving Max an idea of how long such a redecoration might take.

"You could have it ready for her in under a month. Less if she doesn't mind shifting from one bedroom to the other. Would that be soon enough?"

"For someone who doesn't even want to move, I'd say so," Max joked, "although, I believe she'll be more comfortable than she thinks she'll be once we're finished with this place." He realized he'd included Rosemary in his plans and quickly tried to correct himself. "I mean, once I've finished with it."

"You're making me wish I wasn't hurrying off to Cyprus. This is just the kind of project I could sink my teeth into." Rosemary gazed at the faded wallpaper with longing, her fingers itching to begin tearing at the curled edges.

She resisted the urge and looked to Max. "What do you think?"

"I think you are a genius, Rosemary." He found

himself standing close enough to her to smell her perfume. Rosemary's heart began to thump a little harder, and her breath caught in her throat. She took an instinctual step back and was so preoccupied with her own confusing thoughts she didn't notice the look of disappointment that crossed Max's face.

"Not a genius, just an artist with a vision." She struggled to keep her voice steady and was relieved when Max returned her smile. It took an effort for him to do so, but he wasn't the type of man who would allow her to be uncomfortable.

Right now, he sincerely wished he were.

CHAPTER TEN

Dr. Redberry, his wife, and his office were quiet the next day, causing Rosemary to spend an inordinate amount of time agonizing over whether she ought to go over and check on the couple.

Somewhere around the middle of the day, Vera had enough and snapped, "If you want to go over there, then go. If not, stop worrying about it and relax."

Frederick opined—and Vera had begun to agree—that putting off their trip might have been unnecessary.

The men spent the day lounging around, eating, and meandering down by the riverbanks, while Vera finally persuaded Rosemary to spend some money at the stores. An inordinate amount of money, to her mind, though she supposed any sum was worth the smile on Vera's face. What was more, her cases were packed and ready to go, and she'd managed to find a bathing costume that was both stylish and modest enough to suit her tastes.

Eventually, Rosemary pushed her concerns to the back of her mind, and even enjoyed another evening with Vera, her brother, and Desmond. They had reached a sort of understanding, with Frederick and Desmond allowing themselves to be led around by the women, their protests delivered only half-heartedly.

Breakfast the next day started as a gay affair, with talk of the forthcoming holiday dominating the conversation.

"I hear the ruins are rather beautiful and worth a day of foot travel," Rosemary said, her brow furrowed. "I do hope we've packed appropriate shoes, Vera."

Frederick snorted and answered for her. "I would hazard a guess that Vera has packed enough shoes to outfit everyone who ever lived in those ruins. Stop worrying, Rosemary. They do have shops on the island. If you've forgotten anything important, you'll have no trouble finding suitable replacements."

"He's right, Rosie. I've thought of everything, you rest assured."

Wadsworth, with his usual pomp and circumstance, entered the room with his hands full, "Your newspapers, my lady. I believe you'll want to take a look at the cover of *The Herald*." He bowed and made his exit after depositing the items on the dining room table.

"Rosie, does your butler always have a stick up his rear end?" Frederick asked while Rosemary picked up the paper and began to read. His infantile question went unanswered as she took in a sharp breath.

Killer dentist on Park Road—Dr. Martin Redberry suspected of murdering patient. The article went on to state that the death had not yet been officially ruled an accident, and to speculate that since the man died in the chair and the investigation wasn't moving forward, Martin had perpetrated the perfect crime.

The hush that fell over the table wasn't broken until Desmond cleared his throat. "Is it possible there's some truth to the article? How well do you know Abigail Redberry, Rose? Well enough to be absolutely positive neither she nor her husband could kill?"

Before Rosemary could formulate a response, Frederick offered his opinion with another wave of his toast. "Anyone will kill for the right reasons. Straight down to the most mild-mannered person, everyone has a breaking point."

"You might drive me to mine," Rosemary warned, "if you don't stop spreading jam everywhere." Frederick flashed a cheeky grin, but one that carried no true repentance.

Rosemary sat back down, hard, on her chair. "No matter whether it's true, this article is enough to ruin Martin's reputation and, indeed, his entire career. Nobody likes dentists as it is," she said.

"Who is this reporter?" Vera asked, "And where did he get his information? That's what I would like to know. Max seems certain the overdose was accidental."

"Nathan Grint is his name," Rosemary replied, checking the byline.

Frederick sat back in his chair and smiled until Rosemary cast him a disapproving glance. "What, exactly, are you so happy about?" she asked, irritated.

"I'm not happy, exactly, but I do believe I'm the one who expressed doubt regarding Martin's innocence. And here I am, vindicated."

"You aren't vindicated yet, brother dear," Rosemary retorted. "Just because this reporter has his hackles up doesn't mean it was murder, or if it was, there's no proof Martin is the one who killed Mr. Segal. Whatever happened to 'innocent until proved guilty'? I seem to remember that you relied on that adage when it was your neck being measured for the noose."

Frederick ignored the chastisement. "Who else might have done it, then? Who else would have had the opportunity, I ask you?"

Forehead wrinkling, Rosemary chose not to answer but pulled her eyebrows together as she thought back to Martin's behavior at the play and after the police and the medical examiner had left.

"Personally, I think if anyone in that house is a killer, it would have to be Abigail," Desmond interjected, causing Rosemary to stare at him with a look of wide-eyed horror.

"And why on earth would you think that?" she asked, incredulous. "What possible motive could she have?"

Desmond winked. "Just a hunch, I suppose. That woman is hiding something—mark my words."

"You two are both way off," Vera said, siding with Rosemary. "If the police truly believe Mr. Segal was murdered, don't you think Max would have said as much to Rosie? He'd have been here warning her to keep her nose out of the case."

"He did say he expected the inquest to come back with a ruling of death by misadventure," Rosemary said, declining to mention that Max had done just that. "I can't picture either of the Redberrys as cold-blooded killers."

Laying claim to the last piece of toast, Frederick chose preserves over butter and slathered on a thick layer. He took a bite, then scattered crumbs everywhere when he used the toast to gesture. "How well do you know Martin and Abigail, really? Well enough to be certain of

71

their motives?"

Folding the paper while she thought the question through, Rosemary finally sighed. "Probably not, which is all the more reason to have a conversation with Martin and see if I can get a better sense of him."

CHAPTER ELEVEN

"Please, come in." Abigail allowed Rosemary to take her hand and give it a gentle squeeze as she ushered the group into the entrance hall. Frederick and Desmond had insisted upon joining the women for what they gleefully termed "a bout of sleuthing." Out of deference, the two men had promised to treat Dr. and Mrs. Redberry as friends rather than potential murderers. Rosemary entertained doubts that Frederick, in particular, would be capable of keeping his word.

"Martin isn't taking this very well, as you can see," Abigail gestured to her husband, who leaned over in his chair with his head in his hands. "We thought, perhaps, since you seem to have a knack for solving mysteries, you might be willing to weigh in on the matter," she said, a plea in her voice. "Martin didn't kill that man. Even your Inspector Whittington agrees. The newspaper article will ruin us. Patients are already calling to cancel appointments."

Rosemary looked from Martin to Abigail but said nothing. On the surface, Abigail seemed the type of woman who would defer to her husband whenever called upon to do so. Until that moment, Rosemary would not have guessed Abigail possessed the fortitude to maintain her composure during a time of crisis, but that was precisely what she was doing. While Martin crumbled, Abigail stood strong.

Knowing that she would have done the same had it been Andrew in trouble, Rosemary couldn't help but admire her neighbor and pledged whatever assistance was in her power to give.

Martin Redberry's basic personality Rosemary found more challenging to pin down entirely. Having previously seen a display of his mercurial nature caused a few lingering doubts. The man ran hot and cold at the turn of a moment, and yet, Andrew had always insisted a certain amount of distance was necessary before attempting to judge a man.

Attitude alone didn't make the man a murderer, and once again, Rosemary found herself in a situation where she simply couldn't walk away and expect justice to be properly served. Unlike Rosemary's last foray into solving a murder, Abigail was asking her to find a way to protect the innocent. Otherwise, Martin would be found guilty in the court of public opinion.

With the attention of the news article adding pressure, the police might be forced to reconsider the case. No matter how much she trusted Max, Rosemary worried for Martin's reputation—and his freedom.

"I can't promise anything, but I'll do whatever I can to help," she said, looking at her companions with a question in her eyes. Helping the Redberrys meant postponing their holiday yet again, and she felt terrible about it.

Judging by the sparkle in Frederick's eyes, he was intrigued by the idea of investigating a murder in which he was not the prime suspect. Vera and Desmond both nodded to indicate they agreed. Desmond, in particular, not having had the opportunity to watch Rosemary in action, was more than willing to hang around and see how things developed.

The matter settled, Rosemary shifted into investigative mode. "I think the best way to proceed is to treat the incident as if it were a murder. I want you to be perfectly honest and answer my questions to the full. I need all the information you can provide to make sense of what did or did not happen to Mr. Segal."

To that end, she asked the pertinent questions. "Why don't you start with your movements that morning. Don't leave anything out."

Martin's head came up, his eyes darting to Abigail, who nodded in reassurance. Mollified, he leaned back against the brocade and stroked his chin before beginning.

"Well, after our evening at the theater, I had a bit of a headache. I wasn't looking forward to taking patients at all. I'd honestly hoped my morning would clear itself, as it sometimes does. As a rule, we get a lot of cancellations. Not just me, but my colleagues in the field as well. Dentists are widely feared, even though our practices have evolved in recent years."

Simply having the conversation was enough to put one's teeth on edge.

"It may not be pleasant to receive an injection of novocaine in the gums," Martin continued, "but it's better than having a tooth pulled with only whisky for a painkiller. I did an extraction first thing in the morning, and then performed two teeth scrapings before tea."

Abigail shivered at Martin's description, causing Rosemary to wonder if she was as hardy as she appeared.

"I had planned to spend an hour lounging in my chair. Abigail can attest to the fact that she'll often find me there, sound asleep, when she comes down with my tray. Anyway, I received a call from a, er, distraught patient"—Martin stumbled over the words—"and was forced to make a lunchtime appointment. If I'd known he would end up dead..." Overcome, Martin hung his head in his hands once more.

Despite her reservations about the man, Rosemary's heart went out to him. "I know this is difficult, Martin. Take your time. There's no hurry, but you must be thorough. Please, hold nothing back."

"I'm responsible. Whether the police consider it an accident or not is irrelevant. The man died in my chair. If he hadn't been there to begin with, none of this would have happened. How am I ever going to live with myself?" He glanced at his wife for strength.

Abigail took his hands in her own and spoke softly but with conviction. "This is not your fault. You were simply doing your job. No one can prove there was foul play involved."

"Ah, but therein lies the rub, for unless Rosemary can pull off a miracle, no one can prove the opposite, and like my conscience, my name shall never be clear."

Speaking brusquely, Abigail gave Rosemary a telling look. "Then let us pray for that miracle."

"Quite so. Quite so."

"One wonders," Frederick said, playing the role of adversary, "how a potential murderer might stage such a caper. Oh, not you," he rushed to add when Martin's hot gaze fell upon him. "But still, how might such a thing be done, say a soul bent on murder were to enter into the equation?"

Abigail's dagger gaze failed to turn Frederick from the question, and Rosemary admitted she'd quite like to hear the answer.

After a moment's thought, Martin said, "Forgive me, but I cannot fathom how anyone would have been able to perpetrate a crime such as this. The only people with access were those in the waiting room, and Polly—my aide and secretary," he explained. "All of my morning appointments other than the emergency under which Mr. Segal found himself were set up days ago. I simply don't see how anyone in the waiting room could have predicted his arrival."

"Who exactly was in the waiting room, Martin?"

"Two patients, I believe, but I honestly don't know. You'd have to ask Polly about that."

"Were you acquainted with the dead man in a personal capacity?" Proving herself astute, Vera asked the question.

"In passing, though not well enough to predict what possible motive anyone might have for killing him." Shoulders slumping, Martin said in despair, "No one will believe me innocent, and why should they? The death happened in my office, which makes me look like the guilty party. I am the only one who will fall under public scrutiny."

Clearing her throat, Abigail interjected, "You forget

that I was also on the premises, Martin, and Mr. Segal did not die a violent death. Why should a woman not be suspected just as surely as a man?"

Her husband looked up at her with an unfathomable expression in his eyes and snapped, "We've discussed this at length, and you agreed to keep yourself out of it. Why would you say that now?"

"Because, Martin," Abigail said, glaring at him hard for a moment, "it's the truth." She turned to Rosemary. "I brought down Martin's tea tray, even though I suspected he might be napping. I wanted to ensure that he ate because when he doesn't, he tends to become forgetful and difficult. In fact, I think you might want to put something in your stomach now, dear." It didn't sound like a term of endearment.

"You say you did not know Mr. Segal personally. Was he a regular patient?" Rosemary cut in, getting back to the point. Her focus shifted to include Abigail, watching the woman's facial expressions and noting her reactions to Martin's explanations.

"He's come in for work a time or two, yes," Martin replied slowly. "As I said, I don't know him particularly well." His face turned a delicate shade of pink. "And I hate to speak ill of the dead, but he wasn't exactly the most pleasant gentleman on the face of the earth."

Frederick snorted. "Murder victims usually aren't," he commented and left it at that.

"Please recount the events leading up to the death, Martin," Rosemary prompted, shooting a quelling look at her brother.

"Well, he had a cracked tooth that had become infected and was causing him considerable pain. I offered an injection of novocaine, but he insisted upon gas. Such a big man, formidable even, and yet the idea of being poked in the gums terrified him. I agreed, strapped on the mask, began to administer the nitrous oxide, and reached for my forceps. Unfortunately, Polly is still learning the intricacies of dental procedure and had laid out the wrong one. She's a whiz on the telephone and has a way of putting patients at ease, but she rarely sets out my tools properly. For a trained nurse, she's somewhat of a disappointment. Under normal circumstances, I'd have checked more than once before beginning to administer the gas, but as I said, it was a rough morning. I turned the valve off and went to the supply cupboard to search for the proper forceps. When I couldn't find them, I called Polly in and explained to her, again, what's required for an extraction."

"I can attest to the fact that he's telling the truth," Abigail cut in again, casting a look at her husband that had his mouth snapping shut. "I entered via the back staircase with Martin's tray and went straight to his office, as I usually do. As silly as it sounds, I've always loathed the dentist, and I can't even stand to hear the noise of the drill."

It seemed Abigail had married the wrong man if avoiding the dentist was her aim. Some of her reactions made more sense now that Rosemary understood her distaste for dental procedure.

"When I came back out, I could see into the supply closet. It's just across the corridor, and the door was open. Martin and Polly were talking, and he followed her out of the closet."

Martin cleared his throat. "Yes, that's right. I finished

reprimanding Polly and returned to the exam room. When I saw him lying there, I thought Mr. Segal was merely sedated, but when I began to attend to him, it became clear he wasn't breathing. I ran to the waiting room, instructed Polly to ring the police, and then returned to the exam room to attempt to revive him."

"Was the gas on when you returned?" Rosemary asked, making copious notes on the pad of paper Abigail had thoughtfully provided.

"No, it wasn't." Martin shook his head again and stared off into space. Rosemary was sure he was going over each moment of the morning of Mr. Segal's death, and probably questioning his memory. It would have been a routine appointment for the dentist. Or, perhaps, he was guilty as sin and putting on such a good show that even Max had been fooled. Rosemary was beginning to wonder if everyone around her was an accomplished actor or actress.

"That's part of what has me so upset. I definitely turned it off, because I hung the key back on the hook." When Rosemary's brow furrowed in confusion, he elaborated. "It's a new safety measure the company who sells the tanks is trying out. I'm part of a test group. In order to turn on the gas, you need a special key tool. It's actually quite an inconvenience, and I intend to include that in my review. How could he have overdosed if the gas wasn't even on? That's the part I really don't understand. It wasn't as though this was Mr. Segal's first time on nitrous, either, so I can't chalk it up to an unknown sensitivity. It makes no sense."

"It makes sense if someone turned it back on while you were out of the room. How long was Mr. Segal left in the chair?" Rosemary fired off another question without comment, a trick she'd learned from watching Andrew. Her husband had always said that the best way to get information was to catch the person off guard.

"Only a few minutes," Martin answered quickly—almost a little too quickly.

"Long enough for someone to have slipped into the examination room and tampered with the nitrous oxide?" She'd put him in an indelicate situation. If Martin had left the gas on and then been inattentive for too long, the death could be put down to negligence; if he had indeed only left Mr. Segal for a few moments, there wouldn't have been enough time for another suspect to have perpetrated the act. One way or another, Dr. Redberry's reputation and possibly his freedom were in jeopardy, and he knew it.

"It's possible." Martin sighed. "It looks bad for me either way, doesn't it?"

Rosemary didn't answer; there was no reason to. Instead, she went into problem-solving mode. "I'm going to need to speak to your nurse, first and foremost. Are you absolutely positive she couldn't have adjusted the gas settings while your back was turned?"

Martin paused, his eyes darting back and forth as he struggled to recall the details of the appointment that, under normal circumstances, would have been routine in nature.

"I'm positive; Polly can't even reach the hook where I keep the key. She's too short, and she wasn't in the room with me when I left to get the forceps. Even if she had been there, I trust her not to tarnish my reputation, particularly over a man with whom, as far as I know, she

81

has no connection. If someone did, indeed, sneak into the exam room and crank the nitrous up to maximum level, they would have had to leave it on for long enough to cause an overdose and then return the meter to its original position. There simply wasn't enough time."

He seemed to need to work through the problem, but his conviction appeared to have begun to waver.

CHAPTER TWELVE

"I'm sorry about this," Rosemary said, apologizing to her friends after they'd returned to her home to regroup. "I know you're all aching to get on the train and leave London behind, and, I have to admit, I feel the same way."

Postponing was unfair to her friends, and she was certainly looking forward to her holiday, but on the other hand, it occurred to her that this most recent delay would allow her more time to help Max with his redecoration project. The thought made postponing feel like less of a blow, but her friends would not reap that particular benefit.

Her apology went unnoticed, waved away under a bout of speculation about the information they'd just obtained.

"Didn't I tell you Abigail Redberry had something up her sleeve?" Desmond might as well have danced around singing "na-na-na-na-boo-boo." This was the Desmond Rosemary remembered, before he turned into the mature, rational adult she'd been spending time with over the last few days.

"What could she possibly be hiding?" Vera shot him a look of disdain. "You don't think it's a case of accidental death?"

"It's possible, of course," Desmond hedged. "Anything is possible. I just don't find it likely. You're an actress; couldn't you see that she was hiding something?"

"What would her motive be, exactly? In your superior opinion?" Vera fired back.

"I have no idea. Isn't that what Rosemary intends to figure out?"

Rosemary raised a brow. "It certainly is, and I believe there's definitely something fishy going on here. What we need to find out is what kind of man Claude Segal was, and who his enemies were. Someone tall enough to reach the key tool, and audacious enough to commit murder within such a slim timeline. I believe I know just where to start."

She marched to the phone and left a message for the one person she knew would both admonish her and give her the information she needed.

With walls papered in muted forest-green, dark woodwork and floors, and the corners in need of a thorough dusting, it was no wonder Martin's patients found his practice unsettling. The place needed more bright and light to bring the atmosphere up from dismal to comforting.

Polly Calahan looked like she could have been anywhere from a mature eighteen years old to a young thirty-five. She simply had one of those blank faces that made it difficult to tell what she was thinking or feeling, except when she was speaking to customers, and then it lit up—albeit insincerely—like a Christmas tree.

"She's pretty, but only when she smiles a real smile, and that's not often," Vera whispered while she and Rosemary observed the girl from the waiting room. She sat behind a desk making and taking calls, sorting out the appointments Dr. Redberry had been forced to cancel in the aftermath of Claude Segal's death.

"Thank goodness Frederick isn't here. He'd see nothing north of her neck," Rosemary replied.

Vera smirked and raked a gaze down over Polly's inappropriately plunging neckline. "I think that's her goal, and she's certainly succeeded. It's a bit much if you ask me."

Rosemary had seen Vera wear outfits just as revealing, but, to her credit, only for an evening out—certainly not during a workday. Not that Vera had ever worked at a regular job in her life. She felt a bit uncharitable making snap judgments about Martin's nurse, but above many other things, Rosemary valued propriety, which was obviously a sentiment Polly Calahan did not share.

"To each their own, I suppose," Rosemary mused. "We aren't here to judge whether she's dressed appropriately, only to find out what she knows about the circumstances of Mr. Segal's demise. Perhaps her lips will be as loose as her blouse suggests."

Dr. Redberry had been on board with Rosemary's plan to question Polly, not as a private investigator, but as a patient seeking an appointment. She had found that people were more willing to speak candidly when they didn't know their responses were being heavily scrutinized.

When Polly had finished with the telephone call, she approached Rosemary and Vera with the aforementioned faux smile pasted onto her face, "Is there something I can help you with? Dr. Redberry isn't taking patients today, I'm afraid."

Polly wouldn't have recognized Rosemary as the next-door neighbor even if she had been particularly observant. With the office entrance situated around the corner from Rosemary's front door, there was little chance of encountering one another even in passing. Rosemary used the circumstance to her advantage and was thankful when Vera followed her lead.

"Oh, well, it's not really an emergency or anything, but I would like to get an appointment as soon as possible. When will the doctor be in?" Rosemary asked, allowing her voice to waver slightly.

Polly paused, presumably to consider the question, which Rosemary'd thought was straightforward enough. "In a few days, I'm told. Once he recuperates from the shock. There's been an incident, you see."

It was clear the girl wanted to talk about it, not that Rosemary could blame her for that. What did strike her as odd was that Polly didn't seem shaken by the fact that a dead body had turned up at her workplace a mere two days prior. Some people were just wired differently, Rosemary thought to herself.

Vera picked right up where Rosemary had left off, using her acting skills to feign concerned interest. "What kind of incident, exactly?" She leaned in and lit up the room with her signature Vera smile that not even the enigmatic Polly could resist.

"You haven't seen the papers then, have you?" Polly asked. "Mind you, none of what they're saying is true. Dr. Redberry wouldn't hurt a fly. He's dedicated his life to helping people, and what does he get for his trouble? He's dubbed the killer dentist of Park Road, that's what." Her voice held shock and disgust, but it remained steady, much to Rosemary's surprise.

"Are you saying someone died in here?" Rosemary shivered exaggeratedly.

Polly pasted on the smile she reserved for patients. "There's nothing to worry about, ma'am, I assure you. What happened was an accident, plain and simple. People have all sorts of reactions to nitrous oxide. It's not as though Claude Segal was stabbed through the eye with a sickle probe."

"Why are the papers calling it murder, then?" Vera inquired.

"Why, to sell more papers, of course." Polly looked at Vera as though thinking she might be rather daft. "Nathan Grint is taking advantage of the fact that he was in the office that day, and he has a grudge against Dr. Redberry. Nothing he says is reliable, and most of it is outright lies."

"A grudge?" Vera pushed once more, hoping they hadn't exhausted Polly's willingness to gossip. "What kind of grudge?"

Polly pressed her lips together, and then leaned in closer even though they were alone in the room. "Dr. Redberry told him if he laid another hand on me, he'd be sorry for it. The man was always trying to run a hand up my skirt, and that morning, Dr. Redberry saw him do it. He said he didn't abide by that type of behavior, and that this was a place of business and he wouldn't have me put in that position. It was just before Mr. Segal's appointment, and it's the reason I set the doctor's tray incorrectly. Flustered, you know. And then that scoundrel didn't even have the decency to scurry out with his tail between his legs. Made a big show of conversing with old Mrs. Linley, and then, of course, when Dr. Redberry began shouting for me to call the police, he stuck around to see if he could get some dirt for a story."

"It all sounds so terrible," Rosemary said, her eyes filling with contrived sympathy. "I'm surprised you still want to work here after that type of ordeal."

Polly smiled. "It isn't easy to find a post, and this one pays too well for me to leave just because there's been an accident. So, would you like me to schedule you for an appointment? I assure you, you're perfectly safe here, and Dr. Redberry could use the vote of confidence," Polly said, opening a large spiral-bound appointment book. "I've rescheduled everyone to this coming Friday, would that work for you?"

Rosemary nodded and allowed Polly to write her name in one of the little boxes. Her keen eye noted that the date was only partially booked and that the page had worn nearly through as a result of Polly's eraser. It seemed most of his patients had canceled, and Rosemary worried about the future of Dr. Redberry's practice.

By the time Rosemary and Vera left the dentist's office, they'd learned more about the inner workings of his business than they'd cared to, thanks to Polly's uninterrupted chatter. Once she got talking, there wasn't much they could do to stop her. Finally, Vera had claimed, rather loudly, that she was late for a tea date, and hauled Rosemary out before neither of them ever wanted to have their teeth scraped again.

"She's an odd duck," Vera commented on their way back to Rosemary's townhouse.

"You can say that again," Rosemary agreed. "She did confirm the doctor's statement that there were two patients in the waiting room. It's awfully convenient that one of them had reason to want Dr. Redberry to suffer. It's also interesting that Dr. Redberry didn't mention his argument with Mr. Grint."

Vera wholeheartedly agreed. "At least we have a place to start. How are you going to get him to talk with you?"

Rosemary grinned. "I'm going to make him think I'm giving him something he didn't even know he wanted: an interview with the neighbor of the Park Road Killer Dentist."

CHAPTER THIRTEEN

"Come on, Rosie," Frederick whined. "We can talk about alibis and opportunity just as easily in the park as we can at home. I can't stand sitting inside in this sweltering heat."

The weather had turned balmy, the heat rising up to strangle and stifle. Rosemary had to admit that an afternoon spent down by the riverbank sounded lovely, and hoped it would help clear her head so that they could solve this crime and get on with their much-needed holiday.

Vera and Desmond tossed in their lot with Frederick, and even if Rosemary hadn't wanted to go, she wouldn't have gone against the majority.

"Certainly, I'm game. I'm somewhat at a loose end until I get a call back from Max, anyway. Ask Wadsworth to tell the cook to pack us a picnic while Vera and I change our clothes," Rosemary instructed.

"Yes, ma'am," Desmond answered and headed off towards the kitchen to do Rosemary's bidding.

Vera followed Rosemary upstairs, where they both changed into cool summer dresses with floppy hats that would keep the sun out of their eyes. By the time everyone was ready to go, the picnic basket packed and a blanket tucked under Frederick's arm, the macabre feeling of being surrounded by death had lifted, and the foursome was in high spirits.

They enjoyed picking their way through the throngs of Londoners who had also been seduced to the riverbanks for a reprieve from the heat. Umbrellas festooned the landscape, children in various states of cleanliness ran amok, and couples perched along the banks to dangle their toes in the cool water.

"Here, I've found us a spot," Desmond called from a shaded spot beneath a tree.

Beneath its leafy branches, several stone tables were set with chess pieces, pairs of players sitting quietly and focusing on their next move. Grunts of annoyance punctuated the relative quiet that enveloped the space, and finally, one elderly man swept his hand across the board, spilling knights and rooks onto the grass.

"Never again, Reginald," he said to the man sitting across from him as he gathered himself together, albeit at a slower pace than his level of irritation indicated. Rosemary watched him bustle off, leaning on his cane, and tried to hold back a snort of laughter.

The man he'd been playing with, Reginald, merely grinned as his friend retreated, and looked to Rosemary's group with a smile in his eyes. "He says that every time he loses, which happens frequently. He'll be back tomorrow, I guarantee it." He winked, then rose and made his way across the park in the opposite direction.

"Anyone fancy a match?" Desmond asked, hopefully.

Rosemary couldn't help but laugh at the expression on his face, half a pout and half a challenge, that reminded her of their childhood together. Suddenly, she felt at ease with Desmond and allowed the trepidation she'd been feeling regarding seeing him again begin to dissipate. Rosemary realized it was becoming easier to let go of her worries and considered it a sign that her heart was beginning to heal. It would always mourn for Andrew, but the wound was turning into a scar and becoming less painful by the day.

"Nope, I'm making a beeline for the water," Vera declared. "I plan to make a spectacle of myself by wading in the shallows with my skirts tucked up between my legs."

Frederick winked. "I think I'll join Vera, but you two go ahead. Unless Desmond has been taking lessons, it'll be a short match anyway." He set the picnic basket down on the blanket he'd already laid out and kicked off his shoes. "I'll race you," he said to Vera and took off before she could ready herself.

"Not fair!" Vera cried, running after him. She looked a sight in her sundress and bare feet, sprinting around groups of people settled on the grass. It brought another smile to Rosemary's face and pushed all thoughts of Dr. Redberry and his wife from her mind.

"Are you ready to lose to me for the seven-millionth time?" she quipped, setting the pieces back to rights and grinning at Desmond across the table.

Desmond returned her smile with a look of mock malice. "Keep dreaming, Rosie Poesy." The nickname brought back another rush of childhood memories but failed to disarm her enough to miss the intention behind his opening move.

They sat, alternately staring at the board and eying one another with suspicion for near on twenty minutes.

"And, checkmate," Rosemary finally said triumphantly, flicking Desmond's queen off the board with a grin and cornering his king. "Rematch? Or are you appropriately chagrined?" she quipped.

"I believe I've been humiliated enough for one afternoon," Desmond said wryly. "How about a walk down by the river?"

Rosemary pretended to consider. "I suppose that would be nice," she agreed when his face began to fall. "I know how much you enjoy feeding the ducks."

Desmond put a friendly hand on the small of her back as he guided her towards the shore, and it sent a thrill up her spine. She didn't know whether it was Desmond himself, or the mere touch of a man after so many months of being alone that had her breath hitching in her throat. Either way, she felt a twinge of guilt even though she knew it was absurd. It wasn't as though she was cheating on Andrew, but it almost felt as though that were the case.

His light conversation put her at ease, and by the time they returned to the picnic blanket, the tension she'd been carrying in her shoulders was a distant memory.

Several hours later, after the four friends had lounged beneath the large oak tree to their hearts' content, it was almost as if none of the unpleasantness of the last few days had even happened.

"I suppose we ought to get back to the real world, hadn't we?" Rosemary mused, reluctant to return to the and even more anxious for their real holiday to begin.

Vera groaned. "Just a little while longer?" she said, and pouted in Rosemary's direction.

Rosemary returned to her prone position and crossed her ankles. "All right, you talked me into it."

CHAPTER FOURTEEN

Wadsworth knocked gently on Rosemary's bedroom door, rousing her from a dream about the beaches of Cyprus, and she answered with a hint of annoyance. "Yes, what is it?"

"Inspector Whittington is here to see you. Shall I inform him that you're otherwise occupied?"

Rosemary woke fully with a start. "No, tell him I'll be right down." She dressed, fixed her hair and makeup, and hurried down to meet Max in the parlor a record ten minutes later—a feat which Vera would chide her for performing.

Max couldn't deny that he had been pleased when Rosemary called and informed him that she wouldn't be leaving on the afternoon train after all. As much as he knew she could probably use a break from the bustle of London, he didn't relish the idea of her on holiday with that Desmond character. Not, he admitted, that he had any idea what kind of man Desmond really was, but the way he looked at Rosemary was enough to set Max's blood boiling. Too familiar and far too appreciative were Desmond's glances.

By the time he had arrived at number 8 Park Road, a realization had dawned on him; her call had nothing to do with social niceties, and everything to do with the supposed murder that had taken place next door. His mood turned stormy, though it didn't escape his attention that he had no right to be upset.

When she entered the room, he noted that she'd got some sun since the last time he'd seen her and marveled again at how easily those blue eyes of hers could pierce through to the heart of a man.

Of course, he couldn't say as much to her, because that might violate the nature of their relationship. What he enjoyed with Rosemary could only be termed a friendship, even though his heart ached for her—had always ached for her.

Rosemary belonged to Andrew, and Max was the kind of man who would never poach from a friend. Then Andrew had died, and it felt like a betrayal when hope flared to life.

For love of Andrew, Max had kept his thoughts and feelings to himself, pushed them deep down and sworn they'd never see the light of day. He missed Andrew more than he could express, and couldn't imagine how profound was Rosemary's loss. These were the thoughts that had swirled around in his head for the last year, voiding the promise he'd made to himself over and over again.

Still, he felt the nature of their relationship had undergone a change in the last few weeks. Max had always been a peripheral figure in Rosemary's life, but when she involved herself in the murder at Barton Manor, he couldn't help himself from becoming an overprotective oaf.

He suspected Rosemary had enough people in her life who cared overly much and cursed himself every time one of their encounters turned into an argument. On the other hand, he also enjoyed the fiery way she reacted to such behavior, which presented Max with a bit of a conundrum.

"Hello, Rosemary," he greeted her, trying to keep his voice from betraying the emotions roiling beneath the surface. "I was surprised when you rang and said you weren't leaving for your holiday just yet. Would that have anything to do with the story circling the papers?"

Rosemary sighed. "You already know the answer to that question. I feel an obligation to the Redberrys for some ungodly reason, and now I'm mired in the mystery of it all."

"You don't have to be. You could just as easily walk away, go on holiday, and forget the whole thing ever happened." Max realized he was going round in circles. Just when he thought he wanted her to stay, he changed his mind and decided she'd be better off far away from this mess.

"They've asked for my help, Max." Rosemary was at the edge of her patience. "Martin and Abigail are my next-door neighbors. Do you have any idea how awkward it would be if I declined? I still have to live here, you know."

"Just how much do you know about Dr. Redberry? Since you're such good neighbors and all," he couldn't help but ask.

Rosemary glowered at him. "I didn't say we were the best of friends. I can't tell for certain what type of man

Martin is. He's displayed behavior of a somewhat questionable nature, but as to his guilt or innocence, I can only go by my instincts. If the papers are to be believed, it wasn't an equipment malfunction, and that means someone killed Claude Segal. Are the papers to be believed?"

Max settled into one of the tufted armchairs positioned behind him, crossed his fingers in his lap, and peered at Rosemary. "Yes and no. More no than yes."

"Thank you," Rosemary said, her voice dripping with sarcasm as she took a spot across from Max. "That makes everything perfectly clear. You told me, did you not, that the ruling would come back as death by misadventure. Has that changed over the course of a day?"

"What I mean is, it's been determined that the valve from Dr. Redberry's nitrous oxide tank was in proper working order. However, that information hasn't been released to the press. At least, not officially. Furthermore, Dr. Redberry won't be arrested, and he won't be charged with murder."

Rosemary gawked at Max. "Well, that's good news then, I suppose, so why do you have that look on your face?"

"Because, Rosemary, on the face of it, there is evidence which points directly at the good dentist. Doesn't it seem strange that the police would stop investigating, particularly a case that has already been made as public as this one?"

She thought about that for a moment and agreed. "Yes, it does seem strange. Why don't you explain to me what's going on here."

Max contemplated whether to tell her the truth while he pulled out a cigarette, lit it, and sent a cloud of fragrant smoke into the air.

"You must have heard the rumors that have been circling since the war ended?" It wasn't really a question; she already knew the answer. After all, Rosemary had been married to a former police officer, and what Max was preparing to reveal had had a great impact on Andrew's decision to break away from the organization.

She nodded, and he continued. "Half the conspiracy theorists in London believe the police force is filled with crooked cops—officers who used the turbulence of war to better their financial position, move up the ranks, or both. They're not entirely wrong about that, I'm sorry to say. Andrew figured it out long before I did. I still maintain a high level of respect for the law and those of its enforcers who are on the level. I don't blame Andrew for cutting himself loose. He had a wife and plans for a family, and he wasn't going to risk getting caught up in dirty politics or putting you at risk."

Rosemary allowed Max's statement to sink in, the implications making her head hurt. Max was trying to protect her from more than just the possibility that Claude Segal's death might be murder. She knew, of course, what Andrew's reasons for leaving the force had been. They'd discussed it, though admittedly, not at any length. At Andrew's insistence, she'd accepted what little he had revealed and trusted that he had his reasons. Now, Max was taking the same stance, and it only proved that Andrew had made the right decision when he turned his back on what should have been an illustrious career.

"Do you have any idea who Claude Segal was, Rosemary?" Max asked quietly.

"Well, no, I suppose not," she replied uneasily.

"He was a notorious kingpin in the underground gambling market, with connections both below- and above-board."

She connected the dots easily enough. "He had one of your officers on the take."

Max nodded. "At least one, including my chief inspector. That's what I've gathered based on the direction this investigation is taking. Or rather, lack of investigation. Those of us who take pride in our jobs—we who did not allow the tragedies of war to sway us—have been trying to eradicate the crooked amongst us, but it's been a long, hard road, and we've not managed to clear the treachery just yet. The roots of corruption run deep, and in the course of investigating Segal's death, things will come to light that some would rather leave buried. Technically, the case is closed, and whether he's guilty or not, Martin won't be arrested," Max reiterated. "That doesn't sit well with me because I'd prefer to know the truth of the matter, but there are others who have too much to lose. There's only so much I can do without putting myself in the crossfire."

What a hornets' nest she'd stirred up. Rosemary considered her options and thought about backing away from the Redberrys, leaving for her holiday, and hoping things had returned to normal before she returned.

In other words, taking the easy way out. From what Max was saying, the world might be a better place without this particular victim in it, and perhaps some form of justice already had been served. Except he'd been murdered, and Rosemary could not abide the idea of vigilante justice. It bothered her to admit it, and she wouldn't say as much to Max, but it was time to explore the possibility that Martin or Abigail might be guilty.

"Who do you think did it, Max? It doesn't sound as though you stand by the theory that Claude Segal's death was an unfortunate accident."

Max considered a moment. "I don't really believe in unfortunate accidents. Oh, I know they do happen, of course, but not too often. If your dentist friend knew anything at all about Mr. Segal or had any connection with him outside a professional relationship, I'd be willing to bet he had reason to want the man dead."

"You think Martin owed him money?"

"I think it's highly likely," Max stated. "However, I will admit I might be somewhat jaded. My line of work doesn't exactly lend itself to a propensity for believing people tell the truth more than half the time."

"Your theory would explain why he took the appointment," Rosemary mused, "given how tired he was after the evening at the theater. Martin expressed his intention to spend his lunch break taking a nap, but when Mr. Segal called, he changed his plans."

"On the other hand, Martin might simply have been reluctant to lose business. Owing money to Claude Segal doesn't make him a murderer." Max sighed. "It matters little, anyway. He's not going to be convicted, but I confess I'd like to know the truth of the matter." He ran a hand through his hair, obviously irritated. "Maybe I ought to hang up my hat as well. Put a stop to the sale of the house, move to the country with Mother, and forget about all of this."

Rosemary eyed him speculatively. "If that were what you truly wanted, I would agree and help you pack. However, it's not what you want. You love your work and city life, and you won't be happy anywhere else."

"You're right, of course, not that it matters. If I push this case, I'll be forced out, possibly violently. If I let them sweep it under the rug, I might as well turn in my badge. I'd be just as bad as the rest of them."

Max was forgetting one thing: his ace in the hole. Rosemary cocked an eyebrow at him and smiled. "Why don't you let me work my magic? Before you shoot me down, just think about it. I won't even have to put myself in harm's way. Let me play the wide-eyed ingenue, ask a few questions. I've learned a thing or two about acting recently, and I might just have a talent for it. If the truth comes out, the police will have no choice but to prosecute the real killer. If it's Martin, so be it; justice will have been served, and that's all I care about. If certain facts come out in the process, it's the icing on the cake. Furthermore,"—Rosemary held up a hand to indicate Max shouldn't interrupt just yet, and he shut his mouth with a snap—"your name won't be associated with any of it. Your comrades aren't going to come to my house and try to shut me up, are they?"

"No," Max admitted. "They'd be more subtle than that. It's more about taking bribes, hiding evidence, and turning the other cheek. It's easier to do that in this situation than to dig into Claude's background. It isn't as though he was the only one running the show."

"Then let me help. Let the bad eggs cover up whatever they want to regarding their connection with

Claude Segal and the motive for murdering him—which, by the way, could be entirely personal and have nothing whatsoever to do with his criminal dealings. The suspect pool is quite shallow; it shouldn't take much to figure out which of them did it. Honestly, it's absurd."

Max knew he was unlikely to change her mind, so he determined to watch over Rosemary. Andrew would expect no less.

CHAPTER FIFTEEN

"Would you look at this?" Vera tossed the latest edition of the paper on the table and planted her hands on her hips. "Has that worm nothing else to write about?"

"Grint, I presume. What's he on about this time?" Frederick reached for the paper just as Rosemary snatched it and read out the headline.

"*Killer dentist scrapes the teeth of justice.* Honestly, the man should be sacked for writing such drivel, let alone the utter lack of provable fact." Quickly scanning the article, Rosemary huffed. "He appears to be grasping at straws. Anyone with eyes can see that by the amount of sheer speculation he puts forth."

"Let me see." Frederick pulled the paper away from his sister and then whistled through his teeth as he read. "Who could blame Martin for putting the gas to the rogue. Grint credits the poor sod with half the deadly sins against man and nature, then turns around and roasts Martin on the same spit. The way he tells it, the two men were mortal enemies, and the police are moments away from making an arrest."

Desmond read over Frederick's shoulder. "Good thing you're not letting our Rosie meet the man alone. I, for one, will feel better knowing she's protected."

"Heaven's sake, Des. He's only a reporter. What's the worst he could do to her?" Vera scoffed and then found herself on the receiving end of a scorching retort.

"Write a story that paints her a Jezebel, and smears her reputation from pillar to post for starters. I know that wouldn't give you much pause, Vera, but Rosemary might prefer not to have her good name sullied."

Vera regarded Desmond from under a sardonically raised eyebrow. "Don't hold back, Desmond, do tell me exactly what it is you think of me."

To his credit, Desmond blinked and his face reddened as he realized the depth of the insult he'd offered. He looked for support, but Frederick grinned and shook his head.

"You dug the hole, my friend; you'll have to claw your own way out of it. Rosemary and I have a meeting to prepare for." Frederick ushered his sister from the room.

Having Frederick at her side was a new feeling for Rosemary. It wasn't as though they weren't close; in fact, they were as connected as a brother and sister could be, but since Andrew's death, Frederick had taken to treating her with kid gloves. She was grateful for the reprieve and opted to treat the interrogation of Mr. Nathan Grint as an adventure despite the gravity of the situation that had predicated it.

"I feel like we're going undercover," Rosemary said with a grin that reminded Frederick of her younger, more carefree self. "I'm glad you're here, though I don't think Vera would echo that sentiment. She feels entitled to participate in any activity that involves playing pretend."

"She's quite adept at it; I'll give her that," Frederick allowed. "I never quite know what to expect from Vera, though you'd think I ought to considering the length of time we've been acquainted. The two of you were always quite a handful."

Rosemary swatted her brother on the arm and then linked hers with his as they trekked up the high street towards the *London Herald* office. "I was nothing but sunshine and roses, and you know it. I believe I more than lived up to my name."

Frederick harrumphed but didn't argue. He was thrilled to see some of the life come back into his sister's eyes and refused to say anything that might turn them back to the dull gray of recent months.

"Of course, Rosie, of course." His words held enough brotherly sarcasm for Rosemary to know he wasn't going to allow her complete freedom regardless of his worry about her mental state, and the thought made her feel a little better—a little more normal.

"We won't have to lie about anything," Rosemary said. "We'll present ourselves as brother and sister, and I am Martin Redberry's neighbor, after all. He just won't realize we're the ones pumping him for information until it's too late."

Mr. Grint had been quite keen to pin her down for an exclusive interview once she made the offer. In her experience, reporters were ruthless in their pursuit of a story, and she already knew he fit the description, simply based on his disregard for Martin's reputation without any actual evidence of the dentist's guilt.

Andrew had encouraged his wife to focus on facts, to view any puzzle shrewdly, to employ logical methods while searching for patterns. Because he was a man who also respected such things, he'd taught her to trust her intuition and never to discount her convictions as flights of fancy.

If, as Andrew had said, she was to believe solid instincts were the mind's way of letting a person know they were on the right track, then hers simply screamed that Martin had committed no crime, at least, not purposely. Still, Andrew had also said bias was the death of an investigation, and that some people possessed the ability to deceive even the most astute observer.

Feeling pulled in both directions, the only way Rosemary could see to move forward was to obtain as much information as possible and look for the truth among the lies.

"We can't rule out the possibility Nathan Grint might be a murderer," Rosemary mused. "He was in the waiting room, which gives him opportunity. It doesn't take a genius to figure out how to work a nitrous oxide tank, so he could have had the means as well. What we need to discover is whether or not he had a motive. I don't expect him to come right out with it, of course, but we ought to be able to tell if he's hiding something."

"I'll keep my eyes peeled for anything out of the ordinary," Frederick promised.

The *Herald* office was smaller than she'd expected, and not terribly well appointed. Desks were crammed together with barely enough space to walk between, every surface covered with papers and assorted office detritus, and the acrid smell of newspaper ink permeated the air. It didn't appear that the budget allowed for a housekeeper, and if the state of Nathan Grint's desk was any indication, he couldn't be bothered to undertake the task himself.

"Hello, hello, have a seat." Grint remained seated, which spoke of a lack of manners, and nodded towards Rosemary. "So, you're the unlucky neighbor of a murderer." The fox-faced reporter cemented a poor first impression with a comment that put Rosemary's back up.

With a considerable effort, she bit back a sharp retort, including the phrase *alleged murderer*. Remembering her role in today's little game, she called on all her reserves of patience to arrange her features into a concerned expression.

"I suppose so, although one never expects such things to happen, don't you agree? Dr. Redberry seems like such a mild-mannered man." She allowed her eyes to widen just as she'd done when she and Vera had been trying to squeeze information out of Polly, and hoped she'd mastered the art of presenting herself as an impressionable woman. This acting thing was proving not only useful but also somewhat enjoyable.

In one short moment, Nathan Grint proved he had nary a shred of respect for women. "So difficult for a bright young thing such as yourself to look past a handsome face," he said, setting Rosemary's blood to boil. "To see the monster under the skin."

He might have thought she had no more brains than a potted plant, but he appeared to appreciate her womanly assets if the direction of his gaze was any indication. Rosemary's cheeks burned pink, and Frederick looked like he might leap over the desk and leave another body to be cleaned up. Rosemary admired his restraint when he sucked in a breath, clenched his fists, but remained seated.

"What can you tell me about Dr. Redberry? I see here that your flat shares a wall with his." Mr. Grint looked down at the notes from his telephone conversation with Rosemary.

"Tell me, how many times did you see poor Mr. Segal about the premises? Before his murder, I mean. Was he a frequent visitor? I understand you live alone, so you must have paid great attention to the comings and goings of your neighbors."

Swallowing a snort as she imagined herself as he saw her—mousing around with nothing better to do than twitch back the curtains and watch others live their lives—Rosemary said nothing to dissuade him.

"Not that I recall."

"You must have heard some sort of commotion on the day. Raised voices, the sound of the victim's heels drumming on the table as the killer forced the mask over his face." Eyes alight with curiosity, Grint leaned forward as if to slurp up every salacious detail.

"What a vivid imagination you do have, Mr. Grint. It must stand you in good stead, given your profession."

Grint missed the mild insult, preened at what he considered high praise, and still staring at the area several inches below her chin, pressed Rosemary to recount everything she might have heard through the walls.

Rosemary considered the snippets of arguments she'd heard through the walls lately but had no intention of giving Nathan Grint any information about Martin's personal life. "Mrs. Redberry has a lovely singing voice which she employs from time to time, but I suppose that's not the type of detail you want to hear."

Since he wasn't getting anywhere with Rosemary, Grint tried a different approach.

"You attended a play with the Redberrys the night before the murder, did you not?" Grint turned his attention to Frederick. "I'd be interested to hear your impressions of the man. How did he act? Did you get an inkling of the madness under the surface?"

A wry smile twisted Frederick's lips. "I barely noticed the man if you must know. When one consumes copious amounts of gin and spends a night on the town with the likes of Vera Blackburn, all else fades into the background. He could have killed a man right in front of me, and I hardly think I'd have noticed."

"Most unhelpful. Now, if that's all, I must ask you to see yourselves out. I'm a busy man, you know. Utter waste of my time."

They had not offered the type of in-depth character analysis Grint was after, and he made no bones about his displeasure.

Remaining seated, Rosemary decided there would never be a better opening, and it was time to drop the act. She let the smile slide off her face, snapped her fingers to focus his attention on her face, and pinned the reporter with a narrow-eyed glare.

"What I'd like to know is why your story didn't mention any plausible motive Dr. Redberry might have for committing murder. Was that a mere oversight, or have you no regard for the truth?"

He blinked twice and shifted his gaze to Frederick, who offered no reprieve. "How should I know?" Mr. Grint stuttered. "My job is to report the facts, not conjecture."

"That's a laugh, considering you've printed nothing but conjecture. You appear to know little about the victim, and even less about why my neighbor would want to see him dead. Unless you're trying to direct suspicion away from yourself. You were," Rosemary reminded him, "on the spot, were you not?"

"Don't be ridiculous. I've been cleared of all suspicion."

"As was Martin, yet you continue to smear his good name. As you pointed out, the police are satisfied the death was accidental. It begs the question of why you remain so focused on painting Martin a murderer."

Rosemary stood to look down on him in a challenge. "It seems to me, either you are the guilty party, or you have a personal vendetta against Martin. Would you care to elaborate?"

Nathan Grint shot out of his seat and took his full height along with the wind from Rosemary's sails. With the top of his head level with her bodice, there was no way the diminutive reporter could have reached the tool for turning on the nitrous tank.

Grint read the dismay on her face and grinned. "She's a saucy one, isn't she?" This he directed at Frederick, who bared his teeth.

"Why yes, she is."

"I like a woman with grit." Mr. Grint appraised

Rosemary as if seeing her for the first time, or in a different light than he had before. "Of course, it might get her into trouble someday." He wiggled his eyebrows suggestively.

Rosemary realized with a start that she wasn't going to get any useful information out of Nathan Grint because all he had to offer was speculation and innuendo. She wasn't about to give him anything he could use, either. Crooked cops and a cover-up would sell more papers than a murderous dentist. If only he'd taken the time to do a little actual investigating, he might have uncovered more scandal than he'd bargained for.

"I think we're finished here," she said. "As far as my official statement goes, this is all you're getting: Martin Redberry is a kind man, greatly loved by his wife, and heartbroken by the accidental death of a patient in his care."

Mr. Grint managed to maintain a neutral expression, but it took a visible effort to do so. "Heartbroken men don't make for scintillating news."

At that, Rosemary turned on her heel and marched back the way she'd come. Frederick followed, but not before glaring at the reporter with a warning in his eyes.

"If I thought you meant that crack about her getting into trouble as a threat, you would be looking up at me from the flat of your back by now. I trust that you'll take pains to stay out of my way in the future. And hers as well."

Grint paled and gave enough of a nod to satisfy Frederick, who took his time catching up to his sister near the exit.

"That was unnecessary, but I appreciate the

sentiment." Rising on her toes, Rosemary kissed Frederick on the cheek. "Now, I need you to wait right here. I'll be back in a moment."

As she turned to retrace her steps, Frederick opened his mouth to protest, but let the words die on his lips. Rosemary could take care of herself, and well he knew it.

Under the pretense of having forgotten her purse, Rosemary made her way back through the maze of desks to retrieve it. She made sure to bend in a direction that, though it made her stomach roil, allowed Mr. Grint to ogle her backside.

He couldn't seem to help himself, licked his lips, and made the offer she was hoping he would. "A married woman gets used to having a man in her bed. If yours seems too cold with you in it alone, you have my number. I'll be sure to show you a good time."

Since he'd played right into her hands, Rosemary looked him straight in the eye and spun on her heel so he couldn't see the smile that spread across her face. The time would come when he would pay for what he'd done to Dr. Redberry, whether it turned out his accusations were correct or not.

On the other side of the partition, she grabbed Frederick's arm before he could follow through on the fury that seethed in him. "Come along, Freddie," she whispered. "Please."

Reluctantly, and only because the look on her face was amused instead of dismayed, Frederick acquiesced, though Rosemary kept a tight hold on his arm, and could feel the muscles vibrating with the need to act.

Outside, where the reporter couldn't hear, Rosemary

let go and rounded on her brother. "Well, that part of the plan worked perfectly, though I did make it up on the spur of the moment."

All fired up with no outlet, Frederick frowned at his sister. "Enlighten me."

"I knew you would follow me, and I knew a wind sucker like that wouldn't be able to resist making an advance. Are you still chummy with Finley Hollingsworth?"

Too annoyed to think straight, Frederick took a moment to catch up. "I am, but what's Fin got to do with anything?"

"His father owns the paper, doesn't he?"

Nathan Grint was perfectly capable of spreading lies and deceit. However, if he had the brains to commit this murder, which Rosemary didn't believe, he didn't have the stature for it. She said as much to Frederick on their way back to the car.

"He's not our guy."

Frederick agreed with the statement, but the stormy expression didn't leave his face. "He may not be a murderer, but he might not survive if I ever have to watch him ogle you the way I just did. I have half a mind to round up Desmond and skulk around the back alley come quitting time." He spouted a few more obscenities aimed at the reporter's character, to which Rosemary couldn't help but heartily agree.

Halfway home, Frederick said, "It's looking more and more like Martin.If it wasn't an accident, that is."

Rosemary considered the question. "It's possible, certainly, but we won't know unless we clear him without a shadow of a doubt. I have a feeling Nathan room stared at her as if she'd grown a second and third head. If Frederick's eyes got any bigger, they'd pop right out of his face.

"You might as well come clean," Abigail continued railing at her husband, "and let Rosemary decide if she still wants to help us set this to rights after learning the truth. I tried to protect you, but now we have no choice. If she won't, perhaps she can refer us to someone who can put pressure on the paper to print a retraction."

Rosemary could hardly believe her ears. She'd never have guessed Abigail had any idea about Martin's gambling, nor that she'd stand up to her husband as forcefully as she was doing now. What she didn't want was to allow her admiration for the woman to cloud her judgment. If Abigail, possessed with the level of fortitude she was currently displaying, had kept Martin's secrets under wraps this long, what else might she be capable of doing to protect him?

"I'm sorry, Rosemary, truly," Abigail apologized. "I felt it was my duty to keep quiet unless the information was absolutely necessary."

"I would have done the same for my husband." The statement was true down to the letter, and Rosemary chose to keep any other thoughts that crossed her mind to herself for the time being. "However, you're right. This information changes the circumstances a great deal."

"Are you still willing to help me?" Martin asked, a plea in his eyes when they met Rosemary's. "I swear to you, I didn't kill Segal," he repeated, "but I stand by my statement that I'm not sad he's gone."

It was enough for Rosemary and confirmed what

she'd believed all along. Martin was innocent. She just wasn't sure she could say the same of his wife.

"Yes, I'll help you, though we're at a bit of a standstill considering the lack of viable suspects. Nathan Grint might be a shoddy reporter and a travesty of a person, but I don't think he has the stomach for murder. He's an opportunist—he was angry with you for reprimanding him, and he lashed out. He'll get his due, eventually. I highly doubt the elderly Mrs. Linley had any connection to Claude Segal, so for the moment, it appears that you two are the only ones with a motive. Unless there's someone we've missed—" Rosemary stopped short, realizing the implications of what Abigail had said a few moments before. "Wait a minute," she said, turning to face the woman. "Polly isn't as discreet; what did you mean by that?"

Abigail collapsed into a chair and sighed. "You wouldn't have any brandy on hand, would you?" Frederick jumped up from his chair and crossed the room to the bar cart, poured a glass of amber liquid, and handed it to Abigail. She tossed it back with a gulp and a cringe and set the glass back on the table.

"What I meant was," she said, finally getting around to the point, "she's an insufferable idiot who doesn't know a thing about keeping her mouth closed. Honestly, it took no more than a suggestion that I knew Martin was hiding something for her to crack."

Rosemary wasn't surprised by the news. It hadn't taken much for her and Vera to get Polly talking about the death of Mr. Segal, and they'd only just met her.

"It's better if I start at the beginning. I knew something was going on, but I wasn't sure what. So, I

Grint is going to keep pushing, and Martin still needs our help."

CHAPTER SIXTEEN

Rosemary waited for Wadsworth to answer the chiming of the doorbell and watched as he led Abigail and Martin through the parlor door. She stood and greeted her guests, inviting them both to take a seat. "I have good news," she said when everyone was settled around the coffee table.

"I spoke to Max, and the case is officially closed. Martin is off the hook, and there won't be any further investigation."

"That's wonderful!" Abigail cried, her face breaking into a mile-wide smile. "Things can go back to normal, and we can forget this whole thing ever happened." She seemed quite satisfied until she noticed the furrowed brow of her husband.

"What does that mean?" Martin asked slowly, "That there won't be any further investigation?"

"It means there is insufficient evidence for them to bring a charge of murder," Rosemary explained, "and it will go down as death by misadventure." She had expected Martin to be relieved, but he didn't appear to be.

"What you're trying so hard not to say is that the police still believe I'm a killer."

Unable to deny the truth, Rosemary said, "I don't believe you're a killer if that helps at all. None of us do."

The admission fell on deaf ears as Martin railed against his fate.

"What about my reputation? My business? My livelihood? Regardless of whether the police file charges, I've had a significant loss of business, and without a clear statement of innocence, the papers will continue branding me a killer. It will take months, if not years, for the stench of this accusation to dissipate. We'll be bankrupt in a few weeks." Martin put his head in his hands. "Is there no way to prove, beyond all doubt, I am not a killer?"

Rosemary had wanted to gauge his reaction to the news before informing him that she wasn't prepared to let the case go. It seemed prudent to keep some of her cards close to her chest for the time being, until she was undoubtedly sure he was innocent. One could never be too careful.

Abigail gave her husband an odd look. "I thought we had money in savings, Martin." There was an edge to her voice that suggested the money might have been hers. An inheritance or an allowance, perhaps. It wasn't any of Rosemary's business, so she kept her mouth firmly closed but observed the pair with even more scrutiny than before.

"It's all gone. I'm sorry. I've made some mistakes. We should speak in private." He eyed the group as if he'd forgotten they were there and flushed.

"We can talk about it right now. What have you

done?" Abigail crossed her arms and planted herself as if she'd grown roots.

"I'd really rather discuss this without an audience if you don't mind," Martin said, but there was little fight in his tone.

Abigail held up her hands and shrugged. "I'd really rather you didn't have anything to tell, but we don't always get what we want, do we?" she demanded. "We need to lay all our cards on the table, Martin. Otherwise, you'll be losing more than just the business and the house. You'll lose me as well. I trust that's not the outcome you desire, so it's most decidedly time to talk."

Martin sighed and hung his head. "I was in debt to Claude Segal to the amount of several thousand pounds. I didn't kill him. I didn't. However, when I realized he was dead, I admit I was relieved, hoping it meant I was off the hook. It turns out the man has pull even from beyond the grave. Or, at least, he has people who intend to carry on his business—which means they also inherited his accounts receivable. I had no choice but to take out a loan against my practice, which includes the building. So, you see, without patients, we'll lose not only our livelihood but our home as well. I'm sorry, Abigail."

For Rosemary, the revelation answered several questions; but she imagined that for Abigail, it meant something entirely different. Something having to do with betrayal, anger, and fear.

"Did you think for one second that I didn't know about this already? I'm not quite as oblivious as you believe me to be, and Polly isn't as discreet." It wasn't just Martin who gaped at Abigail's reaction; the entire room stared at her as if she'd grown a second and third head. If Frederick's eyes got any bigger, they'd pop right out of his face.

"You might as well come clean," Abigail continued railing at her husband, "and let Rosemary decide if she still wants to help us set this to rights after learning the truth. I tried to protect you, but now we have no choice. If she won't, perhaps she can refer us to someone who can put pressure on the paper to print a retraction."

Rosemary could hardly believe her ears. She'd never have guessed Abigail had any idea about Martin's gambling, nor that she'd stand up to her husband as forcefully as she was doing now. What she didn't want was to allow her admiration for the woman to cloud her judgment. If Abigail, possessed with the level of fortitude she was currently displaying, had kept Martin's secrets under wraps this long, what else might she be capable of doing to protect him?

"I'm sorry, Rosemary, truly," Abigail apologized. "I felt it was my duty to keep quiet unless the information was absolutely necessary."

"I would have done the same for my husband." The statement was true down to the letter, and Rosemary chose to keep any other thoughts that crossed her mind to herself for the time being. "However, you're right. This information changes the circumstances a great deal."

"Are you still willing to help me?" Martin asked, a plea in his eyes when they met Rosemary's. "I swear to you, I didn't kill Segal," he repeated, "but I stand by my statement that I'm not sad he's gone."

It was enough for Rosemary and confirmed what

she'd believed all along. Martin was innocent. She just wasn't sure she could say the same of his wife.

"Yes, I'll help you, though we're at a bit of a standstill considering the lack of viable suspects. Nathan Grint might be a shoddy reporter and a travesty of a person, but I don't think he has the stomach for murder. He's an opportunist—he was angry with you for reprimanding him, and he lashed out. He'll get his due, eventually. I highly doubt the elderly Mrs. Linley had any connection to Claude Segal, so for the moment, it appears that you two are the only ones with a motive. Unless there's someone we've missed—" Rosemary stopped short, realizing the implications of what Abigail had said a few moments before. "Wait a minute," she said, turning to face the woman. "Polly isn't as discreet; what did you mean by that?"

Abigail collapsed into a chair and sighed. "You wouldn't have any brandy on hand, would you?" Frederick jumped up from his chair and crossed the room to the bar cart, poured a glass of amber liquid, and handed it to Abigail. She tossed it back with a gulp and a cringe and set the glass back on the table.

"What I meant was," she said, finally getting around to the point, "she's an insufferable idiot who doesn't know a thing about keeping her mouth closed. Honestly, it took no more than a suggestion that I knew Martin was hiding something for her to crack."

Rosemary wasn't surprised by the news. It hadn't taken much for her and Vera to get Polly talking about the death of Mr. Segal, and they'd only just met her.

"It's better if I start at the beginning. I knew something was going on, but I wasn't sure what. So, I followed Martin one Wednesday night and watched him go into a bar in one of the less swanky neighborhoods. I'd thought maybe he was having an affair, though I didn't really believe it. That's not Martin's style." She remained faithful to her husband, Rosemary noted. Whether it was due to actual devotion, though, she couldn't discern.

"I didn't want to confront him until I knew exactly what he was hiding, and I didn't dare follow him inside to find out. But then, one day I was bringing down Martin's tray, and I heard Polly talking on the telephone. She was talking to her landlord, begging for an extension because her paycheck had been returned due to insufficient funds. That's when I began looking into our finances and discovered that we were nearly broke."

"That must have been quite a blow," Rosemary said after a moment when she realized Martin had no intention of speaking up to either defend himself or provide an explanation. "How did you find out about the gambling?"

"That part was easy. I confronted Polly. Told her I knew about Wednesday nights, and she spilled. She begged me not to tell Martin she'd let his secret slip; said he didn't even know she knew about it, but that she'd overheard a conversation between him and Claude Segal and connected the dots. Of course, I wanted to out her right away, but I was waiting until it became necessary. I'd say this qualifies."

Rosemary directed her gaze towards Martin, who seemed shocked to learn his wife had been following him around and checking up on him. It was obvious he hadn't expected to discover that he didn't have any secrets left. She wondered if it was a relief or more of a burden than he already carried.

"I can't do anything about the money you owe, but if we can figure out who killed Mr. Segal, the police won't have any choice but to prosecute, and your name will be cleared. According to Max—Inspector Whittington, I mean—they consider the matter closed and will continue to do so unless we force their hand."

The rest of what Max had told her, she'd hold in confidence until there was no other choice. Putting a target on his back was an unacceptable risk.

"The best place to start is the scene of the crime. Was there anyone else who might have had the opportunity to tamper with the tank besides the people in the waiting room?" She ran Martin through the events of the day two more times.

Though Martin had dismissed his secretary as a suspect, Rosemary wondered about Polly and decided she ought to keep her dentist appointment the next day. This time, she would have the opportunity to observe the girl with more knowledge of her character. Something told her she might be able to gather even more information using a direct approach.

"What about the back staircase Abigail mentioned? Could someone have entered from there?" Rosemary asked.

"Martin shook his head, "No, it's only accessible from our kitchen, and we keep the door locked."

"All right then. How much time have you spent with Mr. Segal and his associates? Can you think of anyone close to him who might have reason to want him dead?"

Martin spent another moment racking his brain for

anything that might prove useful, and then slapped his knee and stood up with a start. "Claude had a bodyguard of sorts. Charles Dupont is his name, Charlie to his … friends. One could rarely find Claude alone because Charlie was always hanging around in case things got out of hand. It was he who cornered me the night we all went to the theater. The night before Claude died."

Another mystery solved, and one that even Rosemary had forgotten needed explaining. Now that she was aware that Abigail knew about Martin's gambling problem, her reaction to her husband having been cornered on the street made more sense.

"It didn't occur to you that that might be important information?" Rosemary asked, exasperated.

"It wasn't the first time. Charlie spends a lot of time following up." Martin gave the term emphasis. "Usually, that means someone walks away with a black eye or a couple of broken fingers, assuming they're unable to make good on their debts. Mainly, he likes to let everyone know that he's never far away and that he's watching in case you get any bright ideas about running. He was cordial that evening, though—I got lucky because I wasn't alone. He certainly wasn't going to get physical with an audience of my friends and my wife, but he made it known that if I didn't pony up, he'd make it worse for me later. The only reason I didn't mention it before was because … well … I didn't want Abigail to find out. Best laid plans, I suppose. If you want to find out who had a bigger grudge than me against Claude Segal, go and find Charlie. I'd recommend taking these two along with you." Martin indicated Desmond and Frederick, the latter puffing out his chest in an attempt to appear menacing.

Rosemary agreed that the pertinent thing to do would be to find Charles Dupont, and see if there was anything he could tell them, but she didn't have high hopes. If he had been employed by someone like Claude Segal and did the dirty work required for the job, she doubted he'd be willing to part with any helpful information. More likely, he wouldn't want to implicate himself, and in the worst-case scenario, she'd be putting herself and her friends in danger.

Then Rosemary thought about what Max might say and decided it would be better if he knew as little as possible about her plans. If she could discover information that would break the case, Max could stay in London, and everything would be set back to rights.

Having said goodbye to the Redberrys, who thanked her profusely on their way out the door, Rosemary retired to her bedroom for the evening, followed by Vera. Neither felt like socializing, and all Rosemary wanted was a hot bath and a cup of tea.

Anna rallied to the occasion, filling the tub with steaming hot water and puttering about displaying the same odd behavior she had all week long.

"What is it, Anna?" Rosemary demanded, having finally had enough. There were already too many unanswered questions swimming around inside her head; she didn't need another one. "What is going on with you?"

It was rare for Rosemary to raise her voice to any of her staff; in fact, Anna couldn't ever remember having been spoken to so sharply, and it brought a tear to her eye. "It's my tooth, miss. I didn't want to trouble anyone, but it simply won't stop throbbing. Nothing seems to help. Cook has made several poultices for it, but still, it aches."

"Oh, Anna, why on earth would you keep that a secret?" Rosemary asked, her tone gentler now. "I thought you might be in some sort of feminine trouble, or perhaps that you were looking for another post. This is fixable, and therefore, we shall fix it. Don't cry."

Anna closed her mouth and wiped the tears from her cheeks. "It's just—it's just—do you think I'll have to take the drill?"

Rosemary realized Anna wasn't scared of her and felt a little better for it. "It's possible; however, it can't be worse than the pain you're already in, can it?"

Anna shook her head, but the expression on her face told another story altogether.

CHAPTER SEVENTEEN

Rosemary flopped into a chair when she and her friends were alone once more. She allowed herself to be talked into a cocktail while deciding what to do with the information that had just come to light.

"We were this close to being let off the hook," Frederick said, holding up his hand with the tips of his thumb and forefinger nearly touching.

"If you believe our Rosie was going to walk away from an unsolved mystery, you don't know your sister as well as you think you do," Vera retorted.

Frederick sneered and then turned away from Vera to address his sister. "So, I assume you want to track down this Charlie and see if we can shake him up."

"You've been reading too many American crime novels, brother dear. I think the expression is 'shake him down,' however. And yes, I want to find him and question him. We'll take Wadsworth."

When Frederick put on a greatly exaggerated impression of a doddering old man trying to fend off a thug with his cane, Rosemary nearly threw her empty glass at his head.

"He's more than a butler, Fred. He may look old and worn, but you don't need to be young and spry to aim a pistol. Wadsworth's a crack shot. Anything goes south, and he'll protect us with his life."

"Fair enough," Frederick said, sitting back with a pensive expression on his face. He'd had no idea Wadsworth would prove such an asset, but now that he thought about it, it made sense. Andrew would have ensured his and Rosemary's safety, and planting a butler with a protective streak sounded exactly like something he would have done.

Nobody seemed to realize how much Frederick had thought of his sister's husband, but Andrew had been a good man and a good match for Rosemary. The thought caught Frederick off guard, and he had to blink and take a big swig of gin to avoid letting his emotions show.

"No!" Quiet until now, Desmond launched to his feet and repeated, "No! I won't have it, I tell you. You're talking about Rosemary bearding a possible murderer in his den like it's nothing more than a day at the park. You're barking mad, the lot of you, and I won't have it."

His feverish pacing brought him to where Rosemary sat, and when he settled onto the stool at her feet and laid a hand on hers, her breath caught. He looked adorable with his face flushed and his hair ruffled up as the result of restless fingers tangling there. She remembered him during their tender ages, and how much she'd yearned for him to look at her the way he was right now.

But then there had been Andrew, and when his face swam into her memory, Rosemary set aside the remnants of her childish crush. Maybe someday, and sooner rather than later, she'd be ready for another man in her life, but it wouldn't be fair to Desmond to ask him to wait. That was assuming he even wanted to, and Rosemary would rather not add the complication of knowing how he felt.

"I'll be fine. We'll arrange to meet in a public place, during the day when it's safer," she said, trying to set his mind at ease.

"Segal was killed in a public place of sorts, might I remind you, and during the day."

"Well, he didn't have you, Freddie, Vera, or Wadsworth to watch over him. It will all be fine. You wait and see. We'll go as a group, and I'll even let you choose the time and place as long as it's soon."

With that, Desmond had to be satisfied.

"Come, darling. We'll let the men take care of the details while we assemble our costumes. I mean outfits." Vera could turn anything into an excuse for mucking about in her wardrobe. Rosemary wondered if the size of hers was the thing keeping Vera from coming to stay. Maybe she should offer to convert one of the bedrooms, though knowing Vera, it might take two.

As soon as the bedroom door shut behind her, Vera let out a squeal. "Did you see the way Des looked at you? I wish a man would look at me like that."

"What are you on about?" Rosemary lifted a hand to her own cheek and felt the heat flaming there. "Men look at you like that all the time. All you have to do is crook your finger, and they fall in line like ducklings."

"Ducklings," Vera said, spinning and settling herself on the bed, "are adorable and fuzzy."

"As are some men." Rosemary's dry tone pulled a

trilling laugh from her friend.

"So they are, but not what I want in a companion. Give me a little sizzle and burn. I want someone who makes my toes tingle."

Rosemary could count on the fingers of one hand the number of times she'd heard Vera's voice turn so wistful, and the sound of it tore at her heart. Sisters of the heart, the friends had missed their chance to lay claim to the term by legal means when Vera's fiancé, Rosemary's brother, had been lost to the war. As much as Vera chided Rosemary's reluctance to jump back into a relationship, she was the pot casting aspersions on the kettle's shade.

"Has no one tingled your toes since Lionel?"

"Not as yet, but I remain ever hopeful, and I'm having fun testing the theory."

Charles Dupont was the epitome of a flunky, with thick, rope-like arms and a forbidding expression. However, there was some softness in his eyes, and in the curl of his lips when he tried to hide what Rosemary suspected was a frequent smile that had her doubting he enjoyed his line of work. She realized she might have been overly cautious bringing an armed guard along, but in this line of work, it didn't pay to take chances.

It had taken Frederick and Desmond far less time to find the man than Rosemary had expected, though according to them, the feat had been little more than a step away from a pilgrimage to Rome. They'd managed to make themselves into heroes, even though she suspected she and Vera would have been able to complete the task in a comparable amount of time and without half the fanfare.

Now that she was there, standing in front of the man, he seemed far less formidable than a lackey of the type Martin had described ought to be.

"You were there when Segal died, weren't you, Charles?" She asked, playing a hunch and looking straight into his chocolate-brown eyes.

He stuttered, apparently caught off guard at the pointed question. It wasn't as though he believed women were as meek as many men would like to think. He knew better, had met more than his fair share of passionate, fiery ladies. It was part of the job. He had, however, expected that out of the two standing in front of him, the lady who might give him a run for his money would be the brunette whose eyes flashed with a blatant challenge.

"Yes," he stammered, eying Frederick and Desmond with a wary look. Whether he could take them in a physical confrontation wasn't the problem, but it would be two-on-one, and he had places to be and couldn't afford to arrive spattered with blood from a fight in which he had no desire to engage. He didn't even notice the biggest threat, Wadsworth, who remained in the car with his trigger finger primed and ready. "What's it to you?" he demanded.

"To me? Nothing, personally. However, to my neighbors, Dr. Redberry and his wife, it means a great deal. You either had a hand in Claude Segal's death, or you have a clue as to who else might have wanted him out of the picture."

Charlie let his shoulders drop and looked helplessly at Rosemary. "That list is a long one," he said. "About everyone who had dealings with Segal would have liked to see him hanged, drawn and quartered."

"Can you narrow it down to the people who were in the waiting room at the time of his demise?" Rosemary prodded.

"I didn't see anyone. I was standing outside the window, waiting for Mr. Segal to have his tooth fixed. He'd been whining about it all morning and insisted I drive him. Wouldn't let me smoke in the car, so I hung around on the footway while he was inside."

Rosemary raised an eyebrow. "Why didn't you hang around when you found out he was dead? Wouldn't that have been part of your job description? Or are you only responsible for pummeling the poor souls who can't pay their debts?"

Charles' eyes darted back and forth between the group that was now staring him down. "Don't make the mistake of believing I like what I do. I was stuck with Mr. Segal just as much as that dentist was stuck with him. I took off because I was relieved he was gone. Just thought it was an accident. Didn't realize he was murdered until that story came out. Didn't care, either, if you want to know the truth."

"Why were you stuck with him?" Rosemary's heart had begun to soften for the poor man, though she couldn't fathom why.

"Paid my mother's hospital bills, he did. He put her in a nice home and made sure she had nurses to take care of her round the clock. He didn't do it out of the kindness of his heart. I don't believe Mr. Segal had one. A heart, I mean. He did it so I owed him, and made sure I'd spend the rest of my life paying him back."

It didn't surprise any one of them after everything they had heard about the dead man. Rosemary was beginning to think she wouldn't care if it had been Dr. Redberry who had killed Claude Segal.

"You believe the papers, then? You think the dentist did it?" Vera spoke for the first time, and her voice was just as hard as Charles had expected it to be—hard as diamonds, and just as full of glimmer.

He blushed and shrugged. "Couldn't say. Saw him at the games, but I wouldn't have pegged him for it. Not his style. Was always polite, even when he lost, which was frequently. Not his fault, of course. The house always wins, as they say. It wasn't a front, either. Everyone liked Dr. Redberry. Especially his nurse there, Polly something-or-other. Can't say I didn't envy her having a boss she'd go to bat for like that."

"Go to bat for? What do you mean?" Rosemary's heart skipped a beat, and her intuition told her they were onto something.

"Came to the casino, she did. Begged Mr. Segal to let the dentist off the hook. She said she'd repay him in whatever way he wanted if you get my drift. Didn't realize she wouldn't get anywhere with that line. She wasn't the first one who thought she could get out of owing a debt by flaunting her feminine wiles. Went off in a huff, she did. Something not right with that one—mark my words. Hey, you don't suppose she could have been the one to kill him, do you?"

All the pieces were starting to fit together too neatly, and she wanted to slap herself on the forehead for not seeing it sooner.

Polly could easily be the killer, though Rosemary

wouldn't say as much to Charles. She did, however, leave him with quite a lot to contemplate. With a plea to let them know if he remembered anything else that might be of import, the group made their exit, with Charles, brow still furrowed, intent on watching Vera walk away.

"It has to be him, doesn't it, Rosie?" Frederick pronounced when they were out of earshot of Charles Dupont.

Rosemary shook her head. "No, I don't see it. He's capable, of course. Tall enough to reach the key tool, but I suspect if Charles wanted Claude dead, he would have clubbed him in a dark alley and left him there. He doesn't have the finesse to pull off something like this."

"She's right, you nitwit," Vera railed at Frederick. "It's obviously Polly, the devoted nurse."

Rosemary nodded. "Seems so. However, we have to be able to prove it. Just because she wanted to help him out of a jam doesn't mean she'd resort to murder. Jumping to conclusions won't help us. Tipping her off won't either."

"Well then, what will?" Frederick wondered.

"I'm not sure, but I believe I'll keep that appointment with Dr. Redberry tomorrow. If nothing else, I'll get to observe how Polly acts around Martin. There has to be a reason she would try to clear his debt. Perhaps, she simply didn't want any more of her checks to bounce." Rosemary's voice held enough doubt to let her companions know that she didn't believe that for a second. "Don't you worry. I won't be taking any nitrous oxide. I won't even be sitting in the chair."

CHAPTER EIGHTEEN

"Miss, really, I'm perfectly fine," Anna insisted, her words muffled due to the swelling of her cheek. Rosemary could barely stand to look at her without wincing and was considering dragging her, forcefully, next door to Dr. Redberry's office. The tooth had begun to emit an unpleasant odor, and Rosemary simply couldn't take it anymore.

"You certainly are not fine, Anna. Come now, I will give up my appointment, and Dr. Redberry will take good care of you in my place," Rosemary said gently.

Anna's eyes widened, and if possible, she looked even more distraught. "You want me to see the killer dentist?" she whispered.

Rosemary's brow furrowed, and her eyes turned hard. "I do not believe Martin to be a killer, and you have no need to worry. If you don't want gas, he can give you an injection of novocaine. It's just a little prick, I promise. You'll barely feel it, and when he's finished, you'll feel much better. You cannot travel like that, and you don't want to miss out on the view of the mountains from the beaches of Cyprus, now do you?"

The thought of not going on holiday was enough to encourage Anna to give Dr. Redberry a chance despite her misgivings, and she bowed her head and followed Rosemary and a sympathetic Vera out the door, whimpering during the entire walk around the corner and into the dentist's office. It wasn't as though Rosemary couldn't understand her trepidation; what she couldn't understand was for what reason Anna thought she might become a target for Dr. Redberry even if he had killed Claude Segal.

Gathering every bit of patience she could muster, Rosemary made soothing noises and kept a comforting hand on Anna's back until they entered the waiting room.

"Mrs. Linley, I do apologize for the confusion." Polly maintained a facade of composure, but the irritation in her eyes didn't escape Rosemary's notice. "I have you down for eleven o'clock, not ten."

Mrs. Linley scowled. "You must have made a mistake then, girl, because I have a standing appointment at the hairdresser every other Monday morning. I assure you, I made my appointment for ten o'clock so that I could come straight here afterward." Petite and wizened in the extreme, Mrs. Linley still managed to appear formidable, though she didn't shake Polly.

Rosemary hoped that if she lived to the ripe age of eighty and some, she retained half as much sass as Mrs. Linley possessed. Obviously, the woman didn't buy into the killer dentist story that had been perpetuated by the paper, because she had rescheduled her cleaning even though Dr. Redberry's office echoed with emptiness these days.

"I can try to get you in as soon as possible, but Dr. Redberry does have another patient on the schedule," Polly explained.

Rosemary saw an opportunity and seized it with both hands. "Miss Calahan, might I have a word?" she said, smiling at Mrs. Linley with an apology in her eyes. "My appointment is for ten o'clock, but I would be happy to wait until eleven."

The elderly woman didn't exactly smile, but she did cast Rosemary a grateful look and followed up with a steely glare in Polly's direction.

"Of course, Mrs. Lillywhite. I think that would suit everyone just fine. Please wait a moment while I fetch your paperwork. Mrs. Linley, please have a seat. Dr. Redberry will be right with you." She bustled off with a smile, though Rosemary could imagine her thoughts were far less charitable.

Mrs. Linley settled down beside Vera and Anna, took one look at Anna's swollen face, and stood back up. When Polly reentered from the back room, Mrs. Linley stalked over to her desk. "I've changed my mind. This poor girl requires immediate attention. I will wait."

Polly sighed. "That's very kind of you, Mrs. Linley; however, I don't believe she has an appointment."

"She'll be taking my appointment," Rosemary interrupted. "I am in no pain and am more than willing to wait to be seen. This is Anna Watson, but please put the bill under my name. I will take care of it."

Anna gasped and protested. "Oh, thank you, madam!" she exclaimed. "Please, take it out of my wages."

"Absolutely not," Rosemary replied. "Don't you worry about a thing, dear. We can't have you walking around feeling like this, and you've more than earned it."

Nodding, Anna sniffed back a few tears that might have been the product of gratitude, or of fear. "I shall do my best to live up to your regard." In a lower tone Rosemary had to strain to hear, Anna added, "If I live through the day."

"Vera, I think I should accompany Anna for her treatment. Can you keep Mrs. Linley company? I'm sure you will find something in common to while away the tedium."

Taking her cue, Vera said, "Why, there's nothing I would like better." She turned a sunny smile on the elderly woman. "You go on ahead; we'll be just fine."

"It seems the office is full of kind hearts this morning," Polly commented. "Most employers wouldn't do what you just did for her, believe you me."

"Not even Dr. Redberry?" Rosemary inquired. "I have heard he's quite generous."

Polly smiled, genuinely for once. "Yes, you've heard correctly. Dr. Redberry is one in a million." Her eyes went a little dreamy, and it struck Rosemary that Polly might feel some deep personal sentiment towards Martin.

"Anna Watson. Come with me, please." The man in question appeared, and Rosemary followed dutifully behind her maid, whose eyes had widened yet again with trepidation and fear.

"Hello, Rosemary," he said as the three of them trooped to the examination room. Rosemary looked behind her, noted the way Polly stared after Dr. Redberry, and cast Vera a meaningful look. The ball was in her court now, and it would be up to her to garner whatever information she could get Mrs. Linley and Polly to offer up.

"How are you, Martin?" she asked once the door had closed behind them.

"I'm just fine," he replied, giving Anna a reassuring smile. "Let me take a look. I can tell you're in pain, but I promise you'll feel better soon. Open wide."

Polly was right; Dr. Redberry was one in a million. Rosemary recalled the last time she'd visited the dentist—too long ago, she knew—and how much of an ordeal it had been. London could use someone like Martin, and Rosemary felt her resolve to clear his name and solve Claude Segal's murder strengthen even further.

"Unfortunately, two of your teeth are impacted, and it's caused an abscess," Dr. Redberry explained. "I'm afraid we're going to have to perform an extraction. Please don't worry, it's your back tooth, and you won't even be able to tell it's gone once it's healed over."

Anna cast a panicked glance in Rosemary's direction. "I'm not vain enough to care about that. It's the pain that concerns me."

"I'll give you an injection of novocaine, drain the abscess, and send you off to the chemist for an antiseptic. I know it's scary, but it's perfectly safe, I assure you." Martin kept his tone soothing and his eyes sympathetic as he asked Polly to fetch his instruments.

Finally, Anna took a deep breath and calmed down. After seeing the size of the novocaine needle, Rosemary did advise her to close her eyes, and she did so without argument. A little prick numbed her gums, and within a few minutes, Martin had pulled the tooth and stuffed a piece of cotton into the hole. Anna eyed the extracted tooth with more curiosity than concern, and Rosemary suspected her fear of the dentist wasn't nearly as concerning as it had been before.

"Now, no sucking on anything for a few days, and you'll want that antiseptic. Come and see me again when you get back from your holiday, and I'll make sure you're healing properly," Martin instructed.

"Thank you," Anna mumbled through the numbness and the cotton, returning his smile as best she could.

Rosemary asked Polly to escort Anna out to meet Vera in the waiting room and hung back to speak to Martin in private. As soon as she was gone, he asked, a note of apprehension in his voice, "Were you able to find Charles Dupont?"

"I was," Rosemary hedged, "and I believe I might be onto something." She was hesitant to reveal too much too soon. While Rosemary no longer believed Martin had anything to do with Claude Segal's death, she couldn't say as much for his nurse, and the last thing she wanted to do was tip him off to Polly's possible involvement.

Martin didn't press her for information, for which she was grateful, and instead led her back out into the waiting room where Vera was chatting with Mrs. Linley. Her expression was stormy, and the breath caught in Rosemary's throat. It hitched a second time when she noticed the withering glare Polly cast in her direction before watching Martin retreat towards his office.

"You have a nice day, Mrs. Linley," Vera said, following Rosemary and Anna out of the office.

Once they had settled Anna in and sent Wadsworth to the chemist, Rosemary and Vera retired once again to the downstairs parlor where Frederick and Desmond were lounging.

"I know I expressed my undying love for you, Rosie, and a willingness to engage in a little heavy sleuthing," Frederick said, fanning himself with a piece of folded paper, "but this heat wave is enough to make even me feel like swooning. Have you finished wrapping up this case so we can get the hell out of London?"

"And go where Frederick? A tropical island?" Rosemary retorted. "You do realize it's going to be sweltering in Cyprus, don't you?"

Frederick snorted. "Yes, sister, I do realize that. Did you forget that islands are surrounded by water? If I'm going to die of heat stroke, it might as well be while watching scantily clad women sunbathe."

"You are a pig," Rosemary declared and turned her attention towards Vera, who appeared ready to burst. Her face had turned a less-than-delicate shade of red, and steam threatened to pour out of her ears. "Now, let poor Vera tell us what she discovered during her conversation with Mrs. Linley before she implodes."

"I have only broken this case wide open, but please, let us continue to discuss the effects of bathing costumes on Frederick's libido instead. I am all ears." Chin at a haughty angle, eyes blazing, Vera refused to spill until Frederick groveled to her satisfaction.

"Our Miss Polly is something of a dark horse," she announced in a dramatic tone. "The astute Mrs. Linley noticed our perky receptionist wearing the pin of her alma mater, and you'll never guess what school it was.

Not in a million years."

With that, she settled back and refused to answer until her companions made their guesses. Eventually, she offered a clue.

"Mrs. Linley and I share a common interest. An interest which she has expressed by becoming a patron of the arts and hosting students of a certain academy in her home. One of those students is someone we all know and despise."

Pieces of the puzzle clicked into place for Rosemary, though Frederick and Desmond appeared perplexed.

"Both Polly and Jennie Bryer went to The Guildhall School." Putting the two side by side in her mind, Rosemary calculated their ages. "At the same time."

"Ding ding. Rosemary wins the prize, but there's more to tell. Frederick, be a dear and see if Wadsworth has a tea tray at the ready. I'm positively parched. Mrs. Linley practically talked my ear off. The woman is an inveterate gossip."

A few minutes later, Vera grinned over her teacup and continued her story. "Now, according to Mrs. L, Polly gives Abigail the evil eye whenever she thinks no one is looking, but she smiles at Martin like he's the cat's particulars. What do you think of that?"

"I saw some of that for myself today," Rosemary mused. "If you ask me, she's completely gone on the man."

"Enough to bump off old Segal for him? But she's a woman." Unaccustomed to seeing the seedier side of life, Desmond had trouble picturing any woman as a killer. "Do women kill so easily?"

Vera spared him a sympathetic look, then added to her

story. "Now, for the pièce de résistance: Polly was the last person to see Claude Segal alive. Mrs. Linley saw Martin cross into the storeroom."

"Yes." Frederick set his cup down with a rattle. "If I remember correctly, he said he turned off the gas, then called Polly into the storeroom to show her how to set up the tray with the proper implements because she'd left something off. This isn't news, Vera," he chided.

"If you're quite finished, what I was going to say was that Martin had already specified what he wanted on the tray, and in great detail, when he sent Polly to the storeroom the first time."

Apparently, the distinction was lost on Frederick for he interrupted again, and argued, "And she forgot to add one of the doodads he uses to torture the innocent, and when the lack was discovered, he turned off the gas and called her in to show her the error of her ways."

"Frederick Woolridge, will you please shut up for once in your miserable life. Mrs. L. swears she saw some sort of metal device sticking out of Polly's pocket."

Several minutes of discussion followed, most of which flowed past Rosemary as she turned everything she'd learned over and over in her mind. Eventually, she came to herself and asked Vera to repeat everything Mrs. Linley had said about Polly and her connection to The Guildhall School.

"You know what this means, don't you?" she said when Vera had finished.

Even when she grimaced as she did now, Vera couldn't have looked less than lovely. "It means," she sighed loudly, "that you want me to make nice with

Jennie Bryer."

CHAPTER NINETEEN

Vera had never looked quite so contrite or quite as irritated as she did when she agreed to make peace with Jennie Bryer. Nonetheless, she agreed with Rosemary that an amount of groveling was in order if they were going to discover what sort of skeletons were hiding in Polly Calahan's cupboard.

She was even more chagrined when the address she'd wheedled out of one of her contacts at the theater turned out to be a dank, dark flat just a little too close to the wrong side of town.

"Jennie Bryer lives here?" Vera asked, her voice breathy. "I suppose I shouldn't have given her such a hard time." Admitting she was wrong wasn't one of Vera's strong suits, though when forced to do so, she rose to the occasion admirably.

As they wound their way up a battered, somewhat shaky staircase to the third floor, neither Rosemary nor Vera said anything. Their thoughts, on this occasion, took the same serpentine route from pity-lined sympathy to thankfulness for their good fortunes. The last, they'd keep to themselves, recalling the heat with which Jennie had delivered her comeuppance speech to Vera on the night of the show.

"Well, here goes nothing." Vera took a deep breath as she raised her hand to knock on Jennie's door. "I almost hope she isn't home."

She was, and they heard a loud thump, the sound of something crashing to the floor, and an unladylike expletive before the door opened to reveal a disheveled and irritated Jennie. An irritated and thoroughly shocked Jennie, who gaped at Vera before pulling the door closed behind her.

"What are you doing here? It wasn't enough for you to mock my opening night performance in front of the entire cast, but now you've decided to come and berate me in my own home?" Jennie's voice had turned hard and cold, and had she anything whatsoever to do with Mr. Segal's death, Rosemary would have pegged her as a suspect without a second thought. She looked as though she was capable of committing murder; she might even have been plotting one at that very moment.

Rosemary watched as Vera bit back a sharp retort; it didn't matter how sorry she might feel for the girl, the fire in her rose to the surface anyway.

"We didn't come to berate you, Jennie," she said, her voice more controlled than expected. "I wanted to apologize for what happened the other night. It wasn't fair of me to treat you disrespectfully. You won the part, fair and square." It was all she could manage.

Jennie's eyes narrowed. "You expect me to believe that you came all the way down here to apologize? I know you think I'm some dimwitted fool, but I'm smarter than that, Vera Blackburn." It appeared Jennie wasn't going to accept the olive branch, and really, who could blame her?

"You're right," Vera made a quick decision and laid her cards on the table. "I've come to do more than apologize. We need your help. It's a matter of life and death. Literally." Though she could have acted her way out of the situation, there was no need because what Vera had said was the truth. The sincerity in her tone seemed to sway Jennie, or perhaps she was merely intrigued.

"Go on," she said and waited.

Vera's eyes flicked towards the door. "It would be better if we discussed the matter somewhere more private."

"This had better be good." Jennie's eyes flashed before she turned and led them into her flat. Upon further inspection, the interior wasn't quite as bad as the corridor had suggested. Plants littered nearly every surface and, combined with the tapestries that lined the walls to hide cracked plaster, invoked a romantic feel that was quite soothing. Not, of course, that Vera would have voiced the opinion out loud, and Rosemary followed suit if only to appease her dearest friend.

Jennie waved a hand to indicate they should take a seat but didn't offer any refreshment as would have been the polite thing to do. This wasn't a social call, and it seemed she wanted to keep it that way.

"My friend Rosemary, here," Vera said with a hasty wave in Rosemary's direction, "has a neighbor who is accused of murdering one of his patients."

"He's a dentist on Park Road," Rosemary interjected. "You've probably read about him in the newspapers."

Nodding, Jennie still appeared confused. "I have, but what does that have to do with me? Moreover, why would I want to help a murderer?"

"We're not asking you to help a murderer," Vera snapped. "we're asking you to help exonerate an innocent man. We believe you know his nurse. You might have gone to school with her. Polly Calahan. Does that name ring a bell?"

With wide eyes, Jennie peered at Vera, seeming to enjoy her discomfort. "No," she said, "I did not go to school with anyone named Polly Calahan. Are we finished here?"

Vera looked helplessly at Rosemary, who watched as realization dawned on her friend's face. She might have been charitable to Jennie for absolutely no reason, and it made her want to gag right there in the girl's flat.

"Wait for just a second," Rosemary said as Vera rose to leave. "Do you have a pencil and a piece of paper?" she asked Jennie, who rolled her eyes, nodded, and went to fetch what Rosemary had requested.

Squinting, Rosemary thought back to her encounter with Dr. Redberry's nurse. She recalled every nuance of Polly's face, and then put pencil to paper and began to sketch. To Vera, who had limited artistic ability, it looked like scribbling, but slowly Polly's face began to emerge from the page.

Finally, Rosemary held the drawing up for Jennie to see. Eyes narrowed, Jennie's mouth set into a thin line.

"Yes, I know her, but her name isn't Polly. It's Marianna Lancaster." She swallowed hard and sat back in her chair. "I think it's about time for a G&T, don't you agree?" Jennie's demeanor had changed, and it set the hairs on the back of Rosemary's neck bristling.

The girl rose and began to mix up their cocktails, drawing out the suspense while Rosemary and Vera waited with bated breath. Suddenly, she wasn't Jennie Bryer anymore; she was an entertainer with a story to tell.

"Marianna Lancaster was one of the most talented girls in our class. She could have been a star, but she had an ego and a sense of entitlement even bigger than yours." Jennie shot Vera a cold look, which Vera returned in kind.

"We were doing a run of Macbeth, and she got passed over for the part of Hecate." One more pointed look set Vera's blood boiling. "She didn't take the rejection well. First, she spread a rumor that the girl who got the part—Bethany King was her name—had traded favors to get cast. Then, when that didn't have the effect she expected, Marianna gaslighted the poor girl. She short-sheeted her bed; she put peroxide in her shampoo bottle; and she lurked outside her bedroom window at night, scratching at the frame and making noises until poor Bethany was so tired she took a tumble down the dormitory staircase. At least, that was the story our housemother told the police."

Jennie tipped up her glass and took a healthy drink as if she needed fortification to continue.

"The housemother and Marianna had some sort of connection, and we always believed she knew exactly what was going on because Marianna was never punished for anything she did. The rest of us knew the fall was no accident."

Hearing certain similarities in Jennie's tale, Vera had

gone silent, so Rosemary asked, "You mean it was murder?"

"Marianna pushed her, plain and simple. Bethany died because someone was so jealous of her talent and beauty that they couldn't allow her to live. That is what I call a tragedy. Rest assured, if Marianna were backed into a corner, she wouldn't hesitate to do something drastic. You said she's this Dr. Redberry's nurse?"

"Yes, that's correct. Although, not a very good one, by all accounts."

"I believe you'll find, if you check her credentials, that she has no training outside acting the part. It's just a hunch, but I'd be willing to bet a month's rent I'm right," Jennie said.

Rosemary allowed the information to sink in. Now that she understood Polly's history, it wasn't hard to see that the oddities in her demeanor were intentional. She had duped not only Dr. Redberry, but Max and Rosemary as well. "None of us even suspected that Polly—or, rather, Marianna—had anything to do with the murder. She appeared detached and—well, indifferent, I suppose."

"That's exactly how she acted after Bethany's death. We all mourned for the girl, but Marianna pretended she'd never existed in the first place. She's dangerous, but she's also unwilling to face the consequences of her actions. Psychotic, I believe it's called."

"Thank you, Jennie," Vera said reluctantly. "We appreciate you telling us about Marianna. I realize you could have turned us away, but you didn't. I have to say I respect that. Why don't we call a truce?"

Jennie's big blue eyes widened, and then narrowed

into slits. "I'd rather eat dirt, Vera Blackburn. Now get out of my flat and forget my address." She ushered the pair back out into the hallway and slammed the door behind them.

"Well, I suppose you still have an arch-nemesis, then," Rosemary commented wryly as she and Vera made their way back downstairs to where Wadsworth was waiting with the car.

Vera scowled. "It's a good thing she had useful information, or this time, I'd have made sure to break her nose." The threat was an empty one and delivered without the heat of conviction. "What now?"

"Now, I think I have to call Max and tell him what we've learned."

CHAPTER TWENTY

Rosemary was quiet on the way back to her section of London. "What's wrong, Rosie?" Vera asked, jabbing her elbow into Rosemary's ribs to rouse her from her reverie.

"I just can't stop thinking about how there's been a psychotic murderer practically living next door to me, and I never even realized it."

"Well, yes, it's rather disconcerting, isn't it? Although at least it's Martin's nurse and not Martin himself. That would have been even more awkward," Vera declared.

"Disconcerting and awkward," Rosemary repeated, incredulous. "That's all? You'd think we were talking about running into an ex-beau at dinner with his new, attractive girlfriend, not a murderous psychopath working in the flat beside mine."

"Rosie dear, if you're going to continue with this line of work, you'd better get used to spending time with unscrupulous individuals," Vera replied.

"Who said anything about continuing with this line of work?" Rosemary asked, her voice at a pitch Vera judged high enough to shatter crystal.

"Oh, Rosie, come on. You know you can't resist a good mystery, and lately, they seem to be finding you with the regularity of interested gentlemen." Vera couldn't help but goad her friend.

Rosemary was beginning to look as though she were ready to run off to a sanitarium herself, all wild eyes and disheveled hair. "Vera Blackburn—" she began, and then looked into her friend's eyes for the first time during the conversation, "You're having me on, aren't you?"

"I'm just trying to lighten the mood. It is rather macabre, isn't it? You'd think we'd be used to macabre by now. However, I'm determined to look on the bright side. We're going to tell Max about Polly, or whatever her name is, and he's going to take care of the rest. Then, we can be on our way to Cyprus, where the drinks flow freely, and the men are all the color of sun-drizzled caramel."

"That does sound lovely, Vera," Rosemary said, though her heart wasn't quite in it. Her methodical nature wouldn't allow her to focus on the scene Vera had painted until Martin's—and Abigail's—lives were set to rights.

During the time it took for her to ring Max and fill him in on the fact that Polly Calahan wasn't who she said she was, Vera explained Jennie Bryer's story to Frederick and Desmond. Desmond, infinitely wiser than his friend, smartly kept his thoughts to himself while Frederick managed to further infuriate Vera with his opinions regarding Jennie's finer qualities. She refused to glance in his direction even after Rosemary returned to the parlor and settled into an armchair.

Frederick turned his attention away from Vera's sour expression. "I told you she would figure out who the murderer was, didn't I, Desmond?" he said, which only made her even angrier.

"I suppose you think I had nothing whatsoever to do with it? You, on the other hand, have been more concerned with gallivanting around and getting sozzled," Vera retorted, her face beginning to turn a shade of red that only Frederick could bring out.

The two bickered for so long Rosemary, even with her seemingly infinite well of patience, nearly turned on them both. She might have torn them limb from limb if the chiming of the doorbell hadn't interrupted their diatribe.

"Dr. Redberry," Wadsworth announced, ushering a flustered Martin into the parlor.

"I'm terribly sorry to barge in on you like this, but have you seen or spoken to Abigail since your maid's appointment this morning?" he asked with a wild look in his eyes.

Rosemary shook her head. "No, Martin, we haven't seen her." She cast a glance at Wadsworth, who had been watching Martin with the wariness of a man who wouldn't hesitate to protect his mistress should the need arise. He shook his head, indicating that Abigail had neither rung nor stopped by. "What's happened?"

"I received a message this afternoon. It was the bank, important business that I needed to attend to in person. The funny thing was when I arrived, there was no record of the call. When I got home, I found this," he reached into his pants pocket to retrieve a folded slip of paper and handed it to Rosemary.

"Martin," she read out loud. "I can't take it anymore. I'm sorry. Abigail."

"It sounds as though she's leaving me, but it doesn't make any sense." Martin wouldn't have been the first man in the world to react with shock and disbelief upon being thrown over by a woman.

"Abigail has been under a lot of stress lately. It's possible the burden became too much for her to carry," Rosemary said, placing a hand on Martin's arm.

He shrugged her off, irritated. "No, it's not possible," he repeated, his voice rising in volume as he became more agitated. All three of the other men in the room, including Wadsworth, prepped for a possible battle while hoping it wouldn't come to that.

"She's the one who thought up this whole sordid lie." Martin continued to talk to himself, his eyes unfocused on anyone else in the room. "It was her. It was her."

Rosemary gazed at her friends, and then back at Martin, took two steps forward, and slapped him soundly across the face. Desmond's eyes widened in shock that quickly turned to admiration, Vera smirked, and Frederick appeared as though he might start cheering. Wadsworth's expression, however, didn't waver.

"Ow!" Martin exclaimed, grasping his cheek and staring at Rosemary with surprise etched all over his face.

"You deserved that, and what's more, you needed it," she said unapologetically. "What on earth are you talking about?"

Martin crumpled into a chair and dropped his head in his hands.

"Abigail wasn't in the office the day Segal died. At least, not when she said she was. She came down with a breakfast tray that morning, as I had woken late and hadn't had the time to eat. Later, when that article came out, she decided she wouldn't sit by and let me be sent to prison for a crime I didn't commit, so she lied and said she'd seen me during Mr. Segal's appointment. I told her it wasn't a good idea and begged her not to go through with it, but Abigail can be incredibly stubborn when she puts her mind to it. That's why it doesn't make sense."

Rosemary understood a woman's choice to protect her husband at any cost, but there was one thing she didn't understand. "Did your nurse know about this? Was she in on it?"

"Polly? No, of course not. Only Abigail and I. Why? What does Polly have to do with this?"

"Polly isn't her real name, Martin. She's the one who killed Claude Segal, amongst other things. We think she did those things to protect you. Is there something going on between you and your nurse?" Rosemary's tone indicated that it would be prudent of him, to tell the truth.

"No, nothing. I'm a gambler, not a cheater. Though, come to think of it …" Martin trailed off. "You don't think she has anything to do with this, do you?" He held up the note from Abigail.

"I think it's more likely than Abigail suddenly developing cold feet and disappearing. Did you look to see if she took anything with her?"

"No, I don't think so. I—I don't know. What would Polly want with Abigail?"

"My guess is, Polly has developed an unhealthy fixation and would do anything for you. She did commit murder, and that's as extreme as it gets. This note could be interpreted another way," Rosemary hedged, a sense of dread creeping up inside her. Martin caught her drift and nearly broke down again.

"Inspector Whittington is on his way to Polly's—I mean Marianna's—flat to pick her up now. Perhaps Abigail is with her." It didn't seem likely. The woman was smarter than that, and that meant she could have taken Abigail anywhere.

"You won't find her there. Polly, or Marianna, or whoever she is—she's in the office working on a filing project right now. I just saw her. She said she hadn't seen Abigail all day."

"I find that highly unlikely and, combined with the tone of this note, enough cause for serious alarm. Wadsworth, gear up, we're going in." It was all she needed to say. The butler returned seconds later, his jacket a little lumpier than it had been before. "You come with Vera and me through the main entrance. Frederick and Desmond can follow Martin down the back staircase. Be careful, she's dangerous."

They did just that, with Wadsworth taking the first position in front of Rosemary. He kept his hand inside his jacket; she was sure it was wrapped around the pistol he carried there. It was an unnecessary precaution, as Marianna sat behind her desk, sans weapon, humming a happy little tune.

"The dentist isn't in right now, I'm afraid," she said, an odd look in her eyes that Rosemary judged somewhere between denial and insanity. "You'll have to come back another time." The phrase was one Rosemary guessed she'd repeated many times before, and it sounded almost inhumanely automatic to her ears.

"Marianna," Rosemary said the name quietly, but with an edge to her voice. "Where is Abigail?" She could see down the corridor, watching as Martin turned the corner from the stair landing and crept silently closer to the front office.

The girl continued shuffling papers as though it were a regular workday, and nothing out of the ordinary was happening. "My name is Polly," was all she said, but her eyes didn't meet Rosemary's gaze.

"Your name is not Polly. Now, what have you done with Abigail?" Rosemary demanded, her voice rising in volume.

Marianna finally looked Rosemary straight in the eyes and spat, "It won't make any difference. She's probably dead already." Her gaze darted towards the closed examination room door beside which Martin stood, concealed from her view due to its position around the corner from the waiting room.

He tried wiggling the handle and when it refused to budge, revealed himself by stepping around the corner with fury in his eyes.

"Give me the key. Now," Martin demanded, his voice edging on hysterical.

"Whyever would you want to save her?" Marianna asked, unruffled. "I've heard your little disagreements; heard the slamming doors and the angry cries. The walls in here aren't so thick, you know. You'll be better off without Abigail. You'll see." She picked up a stack of papers and tapped them against the desk until the pile was straight and tidy, then fastened a paper clip to the upper corner.

"She's my wife, and I love her! Married people sometimes argue, but that doesn't mean I want her dead!" he exclaimed, inching closer to the desk.

Marianna stopped and stared at him, eyes narrowed. "She doesn't deserve you. What has she done for you lately? I killed a man for you, and this is the thanks I get?"

Martin's mouth gaped open, and he looked around helplessly. Just as he appeared prepped to lunge across the desk and throttle Marianna, a bang sounded from the hallway followed by the sounds of the door being slammed open. Frederick and Desmond had heard enough and had decided to take action.

Whirling, Martin forgot all about the girl and instead sprinted towards the exam room. Marianna let out a screech, stood, and shoved her chair back, where it crashed against the wall behind her. Wadsworth pointed the pistol at her head and said calmly, "Sit down, now, or I'll shoot."

Her eyes darted between him, Rosemary, and the hallway as if trying to make a decision. Wadsworth pulled back the hammer, and Rosemary said, "I'd listen to him. He's serious."

Marianna sat back down and swallowed hard. She closed her eyes and rocked back and forth, hugging herself and humming the same tune as before.

"How did you do it, Marianna? You couldn't reach the key tool for the nitrous oxide tank, and you had precious little time to ensure Mr. Segal would actually succumb to the gas," Rosemary pressed, her voice hard as nails.

The ghost of a smile crossed Marianna's face. "It was easy. I was the one who was here when they set up the tank. There was an extra key, and I took it thinking Martin might lose the original. He's surprisingly forgetful, you know. He would have thought his wife had taken her own life, and eventually, he would have realized he loved me. It would have all worked out just like I planned." She resumed singing, all the fight gone out of her, and Rosemary correctly judged that Marianna would go with the police quietly.

Rosemary's eyes slid towards the exam room door and then to Wadsworth.

"Go, I've got her," he assured Rosemary, and she retreated down the hallway with Vera on her heels.

She was pleasantly surprised to find Abigail stirring when she poked her head around the exam-room door casing.

"She's sedated, but she's alive. The nozzle for the nitrous oxide tank must have malfunctioned because Polly had turned it up to full blast. If it had been working properly, my wife would have been dead long before we got here."

It only took a scant few minutes and a packet of smelling salts to rouse Abigail from her stupor. Adrenaline kicked in as she came to, and she began to scream.

"Hush, dear, everything is all right," Martin attempted to soothe her.

"But Polly! She tried to kill me. She kept going on and on about how you two were going to be together," she sobbed into her husband's chest.

Martin stroked Abigail's back and repeated himself until she calmed down. "Everything is all right now, everything is all right."

By the time Max arrived, Marianna was ready to turn herself over without a fight, and Abigail was over her hysterics. He stepped into the room in time to hear Martin say to Frederick, "Your sister has quite the backhand. If I were you, I'd avoid making her angry."

"I always do," Frederick replied, looking at Rosemary with pride.

"What's all this?" Max asked, ignoring the scene laid out before him and moving closer to Rosemary.

"Max! We got her," Rosemary explained, stopping herself before she ran to him and threw herself into his arms.

Abigail stood with the help of her husband, her knees shaking. "They saved my life. That crazy wench called me down here and then started spouting off about how she and my husband were planning on riding off into the sunset together. I tried to get to the door, but she grabbed me from behind and clamped a hand over my mouth until I passed out. The whole time, she wouldn't stop talking about Martin and how she'd do anything for him. It was terrible!"

It was all the poor woman could manage, so Max sent her off with Martin. "Call a doctor; she'll need to be checked over. I'll be by in the morning to take an official statement. For now, she needs medical attention and then a lot of rest."

There wasn't time for more pleasantries as Max had a job to do, but he pulled Rosemary aside for a moment before getting on with the task of arresting Marianna.

"Are you sure you're all right?" he asked, his eyes full of concern.

Rosemary sighed. "I'm getting really tired of people feeling as though they have to ask me that. However, in this case, I suppose it's warranted. I'm just fine, Max. Thrilled beyond belief that this whole thing is over and I can get back to my life."

If only she'd known how far from the truth that statement was, Rosemary might have collected her bags right then and run off to Cyprus on the evening train.

CHAPTER TWENTY-ONE

With passage out of London booked for the weekend, it turned out Rosemary and company had no hope of exiting the city and embarking upon their long-awaited holiday. Instead, they spent Saturday being carefully watched by a nervous Wadsworth, until Rosemary had finally had enough. She slipped out somewhere around midday, hailed a cab, and found herself pulling up to Max's mother's cottage before she even realized that was where she'd directed the driver to take her.

In the few days since she'd first viewed the property—the few days that had seemed to last at least a month—the men Max had hired for the renovation had been busy. Some of the overgrown planting beds were now empty of weeds and filled with soil. Rosemary assumed Max had left them that way so that his mother could bring some of the flowers from her country home and replant them here. She appreciated the thoughtful sentiment and felt her heart warm to see Max was the type of man who would consider his mother's feelings in ways both small and large.

Being Saturday, the workers were nowhere to be

found, and the house was quiet. Rosemary almost asked the cab to turn around and take her home, but then remembered where the key was hidden. She paid her fare, and once the car had turned the corner, she circled around the back of the house, retrieved the key, and slid it into the lock. There was no denying she was overstepping boundaries, but Rosemary shrugged off the concern and entered anyway.

Inside, the transformation was even more pronounced. Rosemary spun around, goggling at the difference a few days of hard labor could make. Max had instructed the workers to whitewash the paneling, and that alone was enough to turn the front rooms from dark and drab to light and airy. The top portion of the walls had been covered with a muted, flowered paper in greens, pinks, and yellows, and the shelves Rosemary had proposed to surround the picture window had been installed. She could imagine what it would look like furnished and filled with potted plants.

The kitchen, which had been equally outdated as the sitting rooms, now featured a new icebox and range, but the farmhouse-style sink had been preserved and cleaned. Once the now-sanded floors gleamed under a fresh coat of varnish, the place would be nearly ready for Max's mother to move in.

Rosemary was poised to wander down the corridor towards the bedrooms when a noise behind her had her nearly jumping out of her skin.

"I could arrest you for trespassing, you know," Max said wryly as Rosemary whirled around to face him.

She blushed and stuttered, "I'm sorry, I know I'm intruding. I simply had to get out of the house for a while, and I ended up here. Everything looks wonderful." She smiled and made Max's heart melt; not much of a feat, considering it was already the consistency of warm chocolate just from seeing her there.

His feet felt rooted to the floor even though all he wanted to do was cross the distance between them and take her in his arms. The last time he had experienced the feeling, it hadn't worked out the way he'd hoped, and so Max hung back, loathing himself for lacking the strength to act on his desires.

"You do seem to have a knack for being in places you shouldn't," he said instead.

Rosemary grinned. "I can assure you that your opinion is shared by my friends and my brother, though of course, Frederick was chomping at the bit to see a little action when we realized Abigail was in danger. What will happen to Marianna now?" she asked, her expression changing into one of consternation.

"She's been admitted to the psychiatric ward, and I believe that's where she'll stay for a very long time. Most likely, she'll be sentenced to death, which is no less than she deserves. Two counts of murder and one attempted." Max shook his head.

"I simply can't fathom what would drive a person to do such a thing."

"That's because you have a good heart, Rosemary. It's not a condition all people share, unfortunately." No, there weren't many women like Rosemary, of that he was certain.

She ignored the compliment even though it brought the color back to her cheeks. "You've done a lovely job here, Max. Your mother will be pleased, won't she?"

"Yes, it would be lovely if she were," he sighed, "however, I'm not positive it will be enough to soften the blow of losing the cottage garden and all the memories of Father. Life doesn't always seem fair, does it?"

"No, it certainly doesn't," Rosemary agreed. "You're thinking about having to leave London, aren't you? And just as your mother arrives. The timing is unfortunate."

Max thought that unfortunate timing was and would always be a thorn in his side. "Come on, why don't you let me take you home?" he said, afraid being alone in a room with her for too much longer might altogether dissolve his resolve to keep things between them platonic.

"All right, Rosie, spill," Vera demanded once the pair were settled into Rosemary's bedroom that evening. She'd managed to ply her friend with cocktails in the hopes of gleaning some details of Rosemary's afternoon spent with Max. "You didn't leave with Max, but you returned home with him. How did that happen?"

Vera looked as though she was on the proverbial edge of her seat, and if she hadn't just been to the hairdresser for a trim and a manicure, she might have bitten her nails down to the quick.

"There's nothing to tell," Rosemary said, hiding a tiny smile.

"You might be able to act well enough to wrestle information out of a suspect, but I've known you far too long, Rosie dear, and I can tell when you're lying. Now, out with it."

Rosemary grinned and flipped over onto her stomach with her feet in the air. She felt like a teenager, and not only because Vera's presence reminded her of simpler times.

"All right, fine. You're going to get it out of me eventually. It might as well be on my own terms. There's something about Max that makes me feel as though everything is going to be all right. He's thoughtful and caring, and even when he's doing his annoying best to protect me, I know it isn't because he believes I'm incapable like most men do. He gives me the butterflies, I'll admit."

"I knew it!" Vera exclaimed, having had her suspicions confirmed.

"No! That's the problem. It can never be. Even if I were ready to think about another man—which I'm not, by the way—it can't be Max. He would be a reminder of Andrew, always."

Vera sighed. It wasn't as though she couldn't understand Rosemary's trepidation. In fact, she knew exactly how her friend felt. Lionel, her first true love, had been Rosemary's brother, and when he'd died, there was a part of her which never wanted to lay eyes on any of the Woolridges again—particularly Frederick, who looked so much like Lionel it made her heart hurt.

"You were with Andrew for how many years, Rosie?" she asked, quietly and carefully, hoping to avoid a land mine of emotion. "Five?"

"You know you're right, Vera."

"And how many more years do you expect to live? A good many, I presume," Vera continued.

"Yes, Vera," Rosemary agreed. "I see where you're

going."

"You will move on, I promise." Vera had no hard evidence to back up the statement but kept holding on to the adage that time heals all wounds. "Most likely, when you least expect it," she murmured thoughtfully.

Rosemary fell asleep wondering if Desmond had been right about Vera's attraction to Frederick all along. Unfortunately, her dreams included Max as well as Andrew, the two of them dueling for her affections. Finally, just as the sun was coming up, she decided she wasn't going to get another wink of sleep anyway and rose to prowl through the silent and peaceful house.

Finding Desmond also up and about only added to her confusion. Here was a man whom she had adored as a child and fantasized about as a teenager. A man who had only been upstaged by the love of her life, and who now appeared to hold some fondness for her. It was precisely what she'd wanted all those years ago.

Except now, she was conflicted by her feelings for Max. To have gone from entirely closed to the prospect of new love to having two men vying for her affection had thrown Rosemary. She needed more time to figure out what she was feeling, and yet everything was happening so fast it made her head spin. Shaking her head to dislodge the heavy thoughts, she turned to Desmond and pasted a smile on her face.

"Good morning, Des," Rosemary said cheerily. "I thought I was the only one who couldn't sleep."

"I slept perfectly fine, thank you. I have always been an early riser. I only need about four hours of sleep to feel rested," he replied. "Plus, this way I don't have to fight anyone for the Sunday paper."

She held her hands up in surrender. "It's all yours."

While Desmond went to the front doorstep to fetch the paper, Rosemary retreated to the kitchen to fix a pot of tea. When she came back into the dining room with a full tray, it was to find Desmond standing there with his eyes glued to the front page. "Rose," he said, his voice filled with concern. "Look at this."

Setting the tray down, she strode over to him and peered over his shoulder. There on the front page, was another article regarding the killer dentist on Park Road. The byline read 'Story by Nathan Grint', and had Rosemary fuming.

"This is outrageous," she said, grabbing the paper from Desmond's hands and nearly tearing it to bits in the process. "Dr. Redberry has been exonerated for the murder of Claude Segal, the man found dead in his chair earlier this week," Rosemary read. "Thanks to his nurse, who confessed to the crime after being arrested on Friday evening. Sources state that Marianna Lancaster, alias Polly Calahan, also confessed her undying love for Dr. Redberry and that she committed the crime to protect the dentist."

Rosemary threw the paper onto the table and began to rant. "What *sources* is he talking about? We were the only ones there, and none of us would give Nathan Grint the time of day, much less an exclusive." She picked it back up and continued reading. "According to the London branch of the CID, Claude Segal had agreed to come forward as a witness against Martin Redberry, accusing him of running an illegal gambling ring in the city's underbelly."

"Whoever leaked this information is trying to pin

Claude Segal's crimes on Martin, and they're also connected with the police. We need to call Max."

Desmond steamed up at the mention of the inspector, as he'd had just about enough of Max Whittington to last a lifetime. He couldn't deny that Rosemary was right, so he pushed his jealousy aside and nodded in agreement.

"What's the commotion?" a disheveled Frederick asked, entering the dining room ahead of a sleepy-lookingVera and pouring himself a cup of tea while waiting for an answer to his question.

Rosemary and Desmond filled them both in and handed the paper around. "Someone wants Martin to take the fall for Claude Segal's gambling ring, and Nathan Grint is the one who wrote the story."

"I can't say I'm surprised," Frederick commented between sips. "That man is a snake if I ever saw one. The way he ogled Rosemary, I wanted to punch him square in the face. Although, based on what she did to Martin the other day, my sister can probably take care of herself well enough."

"This isn't funny, Freddie. We agreed to help the Redberrys, even putting off our holiday to do so. And now it seems we've done more harm than good. If we had just kept our noses out of it, eventually things would have died down."

"Except," Vera interjected, "there would be a murderous psychopath working next door, and Abigail would be dead."

Rosemary couldn't deny that was true and decided it was best not to dwell on what might have been. "The article goes on to state that the police are investigating Martin, and to assure the public that he will be held accountable for his crimes. We're going to have a lynch mob on our hands if we don't do something, quickly."

"Then that's exactly what we'll do," Vera declared.

CHAPTER TWENTY-TWO

"And here we find ourselves again, sitting around discussing the state of my reputation." Martin shook his head and looked around Rosemary's sitting room, his gaze finally landing on his wife. "I'm so sorry, Abigail. I got us into this mess. It's all my fault!"

Abigail locked eyes with Rosemary before turning to her husband, and what Rosemary saw there was a thin coat of compassion that, to Martin, who desperately needed to accept it, completely concealed the emotions lurking underneath. Rosemary almost felt sorry for him, because she suspected Abigail's irritation and anger might hibernate, lying in wait for a moment when reminding him of his sins would prove most beneficial to his wife.

It was nothing less than he deserved. However, what he did not deserve was the reputation the deplorable Nathan Grint's article had foisted onto him, and for that, Rosemary wanted someone to pay, and dearly.

"I know you're sorry, Martin," Abigail said a touch more harshly than she'd intended, "but we don't have time for apologies right now. We have to figure out what to do."

"And what do you suggest, Abigail?" Martin barked. Having received the hint that she wasn't pleased with him, he allowed his frayed nerves to push him out of contrition and into agitation.

Abigail, proving wrong Rosemary's assumption of her patience, wound up a saucy response and let it loose while Frederick leaned forward in his chair, taking in the scene as though he were back in the stalls at The Globe. "Now I have to figure out how to get you out of this mess, do I?"

Martin's face turned the color of ripe eggplant, but before he could open his mouth, Rosemary shouted, "That's enough! You two are worse than children, and we simply do not have time for your bickering. Abigail, he made a mistake—a great many mistakes by the sounds of it—but if you don't want him to go to jail for a crime he didn't commit, it's imperative that you let go of the anger."

Rosemary turned to Martin. "And you have no choice but to understand that your wife feels betrayed and that she's angry with you. It's going to take her more than an afternoon and an 'I'm sorry' for her to forgive you. However, all of that is going to have to wait. We have more important things to concern ourselves with right now, such as your freedom and your reputation."

Properly chagrined, the couple ceased arguing and didn't say another word until the doorbell rang and Wadsworth ushered Max into the room.

Rosemary wasted no time with pleasantries and got straight to the point. "Max, thank goodness you're here. Perhaps you can enlighten us as to how Nathan Grint acquired a detailed description of Marianna's confession."

Max, upon further inspection, appeared pale and drawn. "I don't know, exactly, though I have my suspicions. Remember my chief inspector, the one who wants to have me transferred out of London under the guise of a promotion? I think it's highly likely he had something to do with it. Nothing goes on inside the department without Chief Inspector Crowley's okay."

"Which means we won't have the support of the police force," Frederick said, connecting the dots. "Surprise, surprise."

"It's not the entire force," Max clarified. "It's not even most of the force, but you know what they say: one bad apple spoils the whole bunch. Especially when that apple is hiding below the surface, rotting everything from the inside."

"Then what do we do?" Martin finally spoke up.

With a sigh, Max slumped into a chair and looked around helplessly. "We prove you weren't involved in the gambling ring, other than in your capacity as a participant."

"Couldn't I still be fined for that?"

Max grimaced. "Yes, but I'd say it's a better punishment than imprisonment."

Martin couldn't argue the point.

Desmond, who had done little more than thoughtfully observe, finally spoke up. "Claude Segal would have kept records. Not only would it be necessary to keep his accounts straight, but men like that usually consider leverage a valuable asset. My guess is, we could kill two birds with one stone." His eyes met Max's, and he nodded once.

Rosemary caught his meaning. "You think we could exonerate Martin—for good, this time—and prove that the commander was taking bribes in exchange for looking the other way, simply by getting our hands on Claude's record book?"

"It's possible," Max said slowly. "In fact, I think it's the most viable option we have. The only problem is, it's too dangerous. Actually, that isn't the only problem. It would be an illegal search and seizure, even if we were able to get in. Which, we can't, since Martin is no longer a welcomed member of the club, so to speak."

"That's where you're wrong, Inspector," Martin interjected. "Anyone can get in if they know the answer to the secret question. It changes each week, but I can get the current one easily enough."

"Will we all go in at once, or in groups?" Rosemary asked.

Wincing, Martin looked for a diplomatic answer. "I'm sorry. Women aren't allowed through the door."

Max scowled. "That's a moot point. None of you ladies are tagging along. It's too dangerous."

Vera jumped up from her chair. "Oh no you don't, Maximilian Whittington. You can't just put your foot down and expect us to comply. This is no longer an official police matter, which means you do not have the authority to make all the decisions. Besides, you're going to need us." She smiled a wicked Vera smile, challenging Max to object.

"And why exactly do we need you?" he asked, his patience stretched to the breaking point.

"Why, to cause a distraction, of course. Martin," she

said, turning her back on Max pointedly, "you can't really mean there aren't any women allowed inside. Surely you don't expect us to believe that a group of morally bankrupt men gather together and then sit around looking only at each other? There must be entertainment or, at the very least, waitresses to fetch drinks for all you poor sods."

"Yes, that's right, there are usually a few cocktail waitresses and a singer," Martin hedged, avoiding his wife's withering stare. "Do you also sing, as well as act?"

"Oh, honey," Vera assured him, "not at all, but I can get us in. You leave that part to me." She winked at Rosemary. "Abigail, are you up for a little acting, or are you still recovering from your harrowing experience?"

Abigail squared her shoulders and met Vera's eyes dead on. "It's probably the only chance I'll get to perform opposite Vera Blackburn. Do you think I'd let a little thing like a murder attempt dissuade me?"

"I admire your fortitude, Abbi," Vera said with a grin. Abigail preened at the nickname, still unable to believe she'd found herself counted amongst one of her favorite actress's inner circle. It was almost enough to obliterate the storm of emotions she'd experienced over the last week.

A few hours later, the plan had begun to take shape, and Rosemary only hoped they could execute it without a hitch. This was their last chance to clear Martin's name, and that was only the half of it. Max needed her help, and Rosemary was determined to come through as she knew he would for her.

CHAPTER TWENTY-THREE

"I have two trustworthy constables on stand-by a safe distance down the alley. If there's any trouble, I'll hear it from my post outside the window," Max explained, "unless you would like to change your mind and call this whole thing off."

He sincerely hoped Rosemary would take him up on the offer, but knew the odds of that happening weren't in his favor.

Shaking her head, Rosemary protested, "Fred, Vera, Desmond, and Abigail are already inside. There's no turning back now." It was as he had suspected, and his jaw clenched as he ground his teeth nearly to powder. "Everything will go to plan," Rosemary assured him, though her stomach churned uncomfortably.

"Good luck," Max said, "or break a leg, I suppose, is more appropriate. Get in, get the ledgers, and get out. That's the plan, yes?" He wouldn't have been at all surprised if Rosemary had something else up her sleeve, but she nodded in agreement and took his hand in hers.

"I promise I'll be back before you know it," she said before turning and walking away from him.

She couldn't begin to guess how many favors Vera'd had to call in to get herself slated as Wednesday night's performer at the betting house, but suspected a significant sum of money had exchanged hands. It had been Wadsworth's insistence that he act as Vera's bodyguard, and Rosemary hadn't even thought about objecting. With the rest of her friends stationed around the floor, she felt safe enough but knew if things were to go south, her butler would be the one to ensure they all got out of there with their limbs intact.

When Vera had pressed a minuscule outfit into her hands, Rosemary had blanched, but now that she was dressed to the nines, she realized that a good portion of an actress's character came from looking the part. Silky tassels covered the black fabric of the sleeveless dress, and tiny, shimmering beads caught the light and twinkled with every move of her hips. Sheer stockings and a pair of sky-high pumps in which she doubted her ability to walk made her legs look a mile long, and her kohl-lined cerulean eyes sparkled from beneath a sheaf of jet-black eyelashes. She took a deep breath and breezed in through the side entrance to come face to face with Charles Dupont.

"What on earth are you doing here?" he asked, taking in Rosemary's appearance with appreciative eyes.

"Getting us all out of this mess. Unless, of course, you want to go head-to-head with my armed guard." She indicated Wadsworth, who had stepped in behind her. "You said you hated working for Claude Segal, and I would lay money on the fact that whoever took the reins isn't much better. Now, would you be so kind as to point out who is, indeed, in charge now?" She pinned him with a glare, and Charles held his hands up in surrender.

"Won't get no argument from me. Want out of this mess, I do, just like you said," he admitted. "It's that guy, over there. The one with the impressive mustache. Stay far away from him, if I were you."

"I'll do my best," Rosemary replied, and followed Charles to the backstage area. She could see Frederick and Desmond, sitting at separate tables, across the smoke-filled room.

And what a room it was. Designed to ensure the comfort of its patrons in the hopes of enticing them to bet more money, it boasted a gleaming mahogany bar complete with brushed-brass fixtures and a selection of alcoholic beverages that would have set Frederick's head spinning if his attention hadn't been focused elsewhere. It was a wonder Martin had been allowed entry, though she suspected his financial situation before embarking upon this journey had been markedly different from what it was now.

Rosemary's eyes darted back to the man Charles had indicated, and she watched as he faked a smile and spoke to a group of men playing cards. When he turned away, he allowed his true emotions to show: irritation, contempt, and something she couldn't qualify but judged akin to hatred.

Left alone, Rosemary straightened her dress and prepared herself for what was to come. She peered between the folds of the curtain and watched as Vera and Abigail, dressed in waitress uniforms, tended to the mass of men.

When the curtain opened and Rosemary strode into the glow of the spotlight, she locked eyes with Vera, who gave a reassuring smile. She felt herself relax.

The stage, in all its forms, was Vera's bailiwick, and one to which Rosemary had never aspired. Call her a wet blanket, a wallflower, or even a canceled stamp, it was all the same to a woman content to watch from the audience.

Oh, Rosemary, her inner voice insisted, lie to the world, but never to yourself.

The center of attention was an exhilarating place to be. The microphone felt warm to the touch as if charged with the same energy that vibrated through her bones. Tongue darting out to moisten dry lips, Rosemary let her gaze travel the room until her eyes met Desmond's, and the look in his sent a faint blush creeping up her neck.

The time was now, and a lot rode on what she would do this night, but when Rosemary drew in a breath and gave herself over to the song, everything melted away. This moment was just for her. She put everything into the music and let it pour out over the crowd. Somewhere along the way, she sensed an internal shift as the bands that had held her together during her time of great loss went slack. When she breathed into the sudden freedom, it felt right.

Never, in all the time he'd known her, had Max heard Rosemary sing. Outside the window, he stood under the spell of the smoky passion in her tone, the longing that threaded through the notes, the clarity of her voice. Unable to help himself, he pulled his hat down to cover most of his face, used the password, and made his way into the club.

One look at the stage and he decided she didn't need the spotlight to shine.

The mission receded into the depths as he whistled in a breath, and though it wasn't the first time, fell headlong for the glittering figure on the stage. If his focus hadn't been riveted on her, he'd have realized he was not the only one. Across the way, Desmond looked as though he'd been hit by a lorry and left in the street to die.

Part of Rosemary's allure lay in the lack of artifice with which she approached everything in her life. She sang with an honesty that flayed a man to the soul.

Watching, Vera realized she could have sashayed into the office and walked out waving the ledger in the air like a prize, and not a single man in the place would have noticed. Except for maybe Frederick, though he, too, stared at the stage, if for different reasons. The notion tickled a quiet chuckle out of her, and as the song ended, she gave him a less-than-gentle tap on the back of the head.

"We're up." Vera glanced over to see that Abigail was in position, and readied herself to play off Frederick's lead. They hadn't planned this part so that Vera's reactions would remain spontaneous.

"Sorry, old girl," Frederick whispered as she leaned past him to put his drink on the table. Silk whispered against skin as Frederick's hand slid up the back of Vera's leg and came to rest, cupping her backside.

No wonder he hadn't told her what he'd planned, but the ploy worked like a charm, even if not for the reasons Frederick had intended.

Shocking heat traveled through Vera from the spot where his hand rested to tingle all the way down to her toes. The implications of which were not lost on her, but so unexpected and unwanted as to lend credence to her wide-eyed response.

When Vera screeched, "How dare you touch me like that?" and reddened his cheek with the flat of her hand, she fairly slapped the grin right off Frederick's face.

"What do you expect when you wiggle your assets in my face like that? A man can only take just so much, and then he's forced to act."

As Rosemary slipped off the stage, she wondered if Frederick's frustrated outburst was part of the caper, or much closer to the truth than even he imagined.

"Wiggle my assets?" Vera's voice rose to a high pitch. "Wiggle my assets? You're an utter cad, a travesty." The tray she'd been carrying hit the floor, a fact for which Frederick was later grateful as, if she'd thought of it, Vera might have used it as a weapon.

The next thing he knew, she unleashed pure feminine fury on him, and he had to duck and cover to keep her knee from bashing him in the particulars. As it was, she landed a blow on the side of his head that made his ear burn.

While Vera bared her claws and spit venom at the top of her lungs, Rosemary toed out of the high heels and unclipped first one and then the other ingenious little clasp where the straps met the top of her dress. A shrug and a shimmy had the fake bodice dropping down to cover the beads and sequins with unrelieved black. Glitter and glamour were fine on stage, but this was covert work. No sense drawing more attention to herself if she could help it—or so Vera had said when she'd forced Rosemary into the costume at home.

Staying hidden as much as possible, Rosemary waited

until all eyes were on Vera, opened the door wide enough to slip inside, then closed it quickly behind her. Rosemary's stockinged feet coaxed shushing sounds from the cracked linoleum, and soft as the noises were, they echoed off the dingy walls. Crossing to the desk made her feel exposed, but it had to be done, and quickly.

Barely breathing, Rosemary crossed the pool of light thrown by a single bare bulb and reached for the object lying on the desk. Her fingers only brushed against brown leather before a voice came out of the shadows.

"What do you think you're doing?"

Amid the melee, Max angled himself to watch the door through which Rosemary had furtively disappeared, and counted down the seconds until she might return. They'd estimated no more than a minute for her to get in and out as long as the ledger was where Charles had said it would be.

Meanwhile, Rosemary had one hand on the ledger, the other braced against the desk, and her back arched away from the tip of the knife threatening to lodge between her ribs.

Her heart hammered in her chest, but she fought to keep a cool head.

Letting her voice tremble, Rosemary said, "I'm sorry, I didn't know I wasn't supposed to come in here. I needed a place to sit for a moment, the bright lights dazzled my eyes. They've given me a beastly headache. It's so lovely and dim in here and I only wanted to rest for a moment."

"Play your act to a different audience, chickie. You've got your hand on my personal business." The pressure on the knife lessened a fraction, so Rosemary played up the angle a bit more.

"Please, sir. I meant no harm. The pain, my head—it fairly swims with it." Because they wanted to anyway, Rosemary let her knees wobble and cried out sharply. "Help me."

Confronted with a damsel in distress, the hard-faced man hastily dropped the knife on the desk and tried to catch Rosemary as she pretended to fall. On her way down, she managed to flip the weapon across the desk where it fell behind and out of reach.

She was just about to recover from the fake fall, pivot, and dash for the door when it burst open to reveal Max, looking like thunder. Caught off guard by the sight of him, she waited for a split second too long, and the fall turned real. Rosemary hit the floor, then rolled to dodge the feet of the man whose name she still had not learned while trying to keep her dress from showing more than just a length of leg.

When she finally came to her feet, the room had erupted in a melee of flying limbs as two of old Rock Face's men piled onto Max. She winced at the sound of a fist landing solidly. Max needed help, was her first thought, but she took time to reach for the ledger as a third henchman bulled through the door with Desmond hard on his heels.

"Rose." He looked for her first, but she waved him away as she did Frederick, who came in a split second later.

"I'm fine. Help Max!"

Rosemary ducked under a flying fist, skirted the worst of the brawl, raced towards the door, and nearly bowled

Vera over on her way in. "Come on, we need to put this somewhere safe."

Instead of turning, Vera's eyes went wide. She pulled Rosemary down and away just in time for the burly man swinging a truncheon to miss and take a chunk out of the wall next to the doorway.

Thrown off balance, both women went down with Rosemary on top, and the big man pulled back to deliver another strike, one that would have surely killed Rosemary had it landed.

Already too late to stop the swinging arm, Max jumped in front and took the blow on his upraised forearm. There was a sickening crunch as the bone broke under the force.

With a triumphant grin, the hired muscle raised the club a third time and made to swing.

Thunder rolled through the room as a gunshot rang out. Bits of ceiling rained down over Wadsworth who calmly lowered the pistol and aimed it carefully at the ringleader.

"That will be quite enough."

CHAPTER TWENTY-FOUR

Friday morning's paper was received with far more fanfare than the delivery boy had ever seen. Four people waited on the front doorstep of Number 8 Park Road and practically snatched it out of his hands. He meandered off down the street, shaking his head, wondering why adults so often displayed the oddest behavior.

"Aha!" Rosemary exclaimed when she was through scanning the headline. For once, and for good reason, Nathan Grint had finished the job he was supposed to and reported the truth.

"Chief Inspector Crowley gets the ax," she read aloud. "London police Chief Inspector Benjamin Crowley was fired on Thursday afternoon when he couldn't discount the claim that he had been taking bribes from several underground gambling establishments. His position will be filled by Inspector Maximilian Whittington, who was injured during a dust-up on Wednesday night at an illegal betting house. Chief Inspector Crowley is also accused of slander against London dentist Martin Redberry, who was recently involved in the murder investigation of one Claude Segal—a crime for which he was acquitted—in addition to several acts of conspiracy and fraud. The case against Crowley is under investigation by the CID."

"It seems Vera may have been incorrect when she accused you of contributing only lightly to this investigation," Rosemary said to Frederick, her twinkling eyes sliding to the woman in question.

"He has his moments," was all Vera would say on the subject, but Frederick grinned from ear to ear. The two hadn't made eye contact since their encounter at the betting house, and both Rosemary and Desmond suspected they were in for an interesting holiday given the circumstances.

When Max arrived, he found the foursome, plus Martin and Abigail, ensconced in the dining room, enjoying a long brunch. He did a double-take when he noticed that Wadsworth occupied the seat at the head of the table, an unprecedented grin on his wrinkled face.

"I see you've dispensed with formality this morning, Rosemary," Max said, showing himself to the table.

"Max!" she cried and rose to help him to a seat, taking care not to bump the cast that covered his injured arm. "Are you all right?" She looked into his eyes with such concern for his wellbeing that he had a hard time responding.

"I'm just fine, Rose. Couldn't be better, actually. It seems things have worked out better than I could have imagined. I have the lot of you to thank for that. Unofficially, of course, considering my new position." Max positively beamed with pride. "I get to stay in London, and we've successfully eradicated the top offender on the force."

Rosemary couldn't deny that the idea of Max remaining in London had been a large portion of her motivation for exposing the betting house and the officers who didn't bother to abide by the law themselves. She felt as though nothing could shake her spirits now, and looked around the table at her friends, feeling grateful and at peace.

"You invited him to Cyprus?" Vera asked incredulously when she and Rosemary were alone that evening, watching Anna finish up the last of the packing. The poor girl had performed the task several times by this point and had waved away the offers of assistance that Vera and Rosemary extended. It seemed she was feeling grateful now that her tooth had ceased throbbing and her face had shrunk back to its normal shape.

"Yes, Vera, I invited him. The poor man has a broken arm because of me. He's been given a few weeks' leave, so why not take advantage of it? Not that it matters; he declined. His mother arrives today for a short visit before she relocates permanently, and he's busy overseeing the work being done on her cottage. It's all for the best."

Vera raised an eyebrow. "Are you trying to convince me, or yourself?"

"Miss," Anna interrupted, wringing her hands and appearing very much like a sad puppy dog, "I can't seem to find your sapphire pendant. I've looked just everywhere for it, and it's nowhere to be found."

Rosemary felt her heart drop into her shoes. If she'd lost that necklace, she would never be able to forgive herself.

"It's always best to think back to the last time you had it," Vera commented lazily. "Things always turn up, and usually in the most unexpected places."

"That's because you leave your things lying around," Rosemary said, a bit more harshly than how she usually spoke to her best friend. "I'm sorry, but that necklace is priceless to me."

"I'm sorry, Rosie, really. What can we do?"

"I know I had it on the night we went to the theater—oh, my goodness, I know what happened," Rosemary exclaimed, plopping back down on the bed. "It fell out of my handbag when that director man ran into me. There's no way someone hasn't found it and claimed it by now." Tears sprang to her eyes and threatened to ruin her makeup.

Vera immediately switched into problem-solving mode. "We'll go back and check. It's worth a try, isn't it?"

"You're not even allowed back in the building, remember?" Rosemary said, defeated.

"And since when did we let something like that stop us?" Vera retorted. "Get up off your rear end and stop feeling sorry for yourself. We'll find it."

She was right, and Rosemary knew it. "All right. But how do you propose we get inside?"

"We buy a ticket, Rosie," Vera said as if it were the most obvious solution. Which it sort of was, once Rosemary thought about it.

The pair arrived outside The Globe just before the first curtain call. Vera pulled Rosemary around the far side of the building, yanking on her arm so hard Rosemary thought it might come clear out of the socket.

"Ouch!" she exclaimed, shaking Vera off and glaring at her. "What's the rush?"

Vera declined to answer, instead grabbing a scruffy-looking kid by the back of his jacket and spinning him around to face herself. "Two tickets, now," she demanded before he fully realized what was happening.

"Okay, okay. Didn't need to manhandle me, did ya?" he whined.

"Probably not, but it was fun," Vera retorted, exchanging money for tickets and letting the young hawker loose. "I hate to stoop this low, but we're running out of time," she said to Rosemary once he'd disappeared down the block. She mumbled something about hawkers driving up ticket prices, which Rosemary ignored.

Tickets in hand, they entered and started to make a beeline for the door Vera indicated would deposit them closest to the backstage area.

"Rosemary?" she would have recognized the voice even in a crowd and whirled around to face Max, who wasn't alone. Dressed in a well-fitting suit and tie, he looked so handsome Rosemary's throat went dry as desert sand. A hand was clasped around his good arm, and when Rosemary tore her eyes from his face, she realized with a start that Max was accompanied by a date.

"Max!" she squeaked, sliding her eyes sideways towards the woman and pasting a smile on her face. "I didn't expect to see you here."

"Nor I you. Please, Rosemary, meet my mother, Ariadne Whittington. Mother, this is Rosemary Lillywhite."

Rosemary would have almost preferred if Max's companion had been an actual date; it would have been far less awkward than meeting his mother with absolutely zero advance notice.

"Charmed, I'm sure," Mrs. Whittington said, making no effort to reach for Rosemary's hand. Never in her life had Rosemary felt so uncomfortable, as though she were being judged and found wanting. "I do thank you for your contribution to my new flat, although the wallpaper is a touch too feminine for my tastes." The woman had mastered the art of wrapping a subtle dig inside a compliment.

"She's being difficult," Max said, his cheeks burning pink. "She couldn't be happier, could you Mother?"

"I'm not sure you want me to answer that question, dear," Mrs. Whittington replied. "I'd like to be shown to my seat now. The show is about to go on, and it's abhorrently rude to enter once the lights have gone out."

Max shot an apologetic look at Rosemary before leading his mother into the theater. "Have a lovely time in Cyprus, Rose," he tossed over his shoulder.

All Rosemary could do was stare after them, and it took several seconds for Vera to rouse her. Once again, Rosemary felt herself being pulled along behind her friend. They made it to the backstage area without attracting attention, since all eyes were focused on the stage.

"Here's where you dropped your handbag," Vera said, taking a look around to ensure nobody was watching them before kneeling on the floor to search for the missing necklace.

"I don't see it anywhere," Rosemary lamented, plopping down on her backside. A rustle of curtain and a few thumping steps later, just when Rosemary thought they were about to get caught, Vera's friend Samuel came bustling into the corridor.

"Vera dear, what are you doing here?" he asked, eyes narrowed.

After a short explanation, Samuel smiled and beckoned them over to his station. "Is this what you're looking for?" he asked, holding up the beloved sapphire necklace.

Rosemary could hardly believe her good fortune and fastened it back around her neck, making a silent vow to send a donation to the actors' guild the second she returned from holiday. "You have no idea what this means to me. Thank you," she said graciously.

"Think nothing of it, dear, but please, you two, leave me now," he chided. "I have to be in full makeup for my next scene."

With a nod of understanding, Vera kissed him on the cheek, and the pair retreated back into the theater just in time to hear Jennie Bryer's Titania bickering with Oberon. "These are the forgeries of jealousy ..." she recited, berating the faerie king for his part in the destruction of the mortal world.

As Vera watched with bated breath, the words took on a whole new meaning. It had been jealousy that drove her hatred towards Jennie, and suddenly she realized she had been acting like a spoiled child.

Rosemary pursed her lips as she watched, and said

nothing.

"Hell, she's not so bad, is she?" Vera said, winking at Rosemary and then sashaying up the aisle with a spring in her step.

The End

MORE BOOKS

Can't wait to find out what happens next?

Scan the QR Code below for my newsletter, audiobooks, and other editions.

The Murder Next Door - Emily Queen

BRITISH ENGLISH TERMS

Bin - trash can

Boot (of a car) – trunk

Cheeky - endearingly rude or disrespectful

Cheerio - a friendly way to say goodbye

Cheers - a quick thank you

Chemist's - drugstore/pharmacy

Cupboard – closet

Daft - a bit stupid or silly

Dolt - a fool

Fancy - a verb expressing desire ("do you fancy some dinner?")

Flat - apartment

Footway – sidewalk

Fortnight - two weeks

Garden - yard

High street - main street

Holiday - vacation

Lift - elevator

Loo - the toilet

Lorry - truck

Match - game

Post - mail

Queue/queue up - a line/to stand in line

Rubbish - garbage

Skeleton in the cupboard – skeleton in the closet

Snog/snogging - a kiss

Solicitor – lawyer

Sweets - candy

Tickled/tickled pink - very happy

BOOK 3 EXCERPT

"Death on the Isle of Love" (Book 3 of the Mrs. Lillywhite Investigates Mysteries)

Chapter 1 Excerpt

"Attention, passengers. We'll be docking in Cyprus in fifteen minutes. Local time is seven fifty-two 7:52 a.m. Please be ready to disembark promptly."

The disembodied voice sounded oddly mechanical through the loudspeaker, but Rosemary Lillywhite caught the gist of the statement. With barely contained excitement, she exchanged grins with her best friend—one of her three traveling companions—who stood alongside her on the deck, waiting for their destination to come into view.

That Vera Blackburn had joined her on this tropical adventure wasn't surprising; the beautiful, spunky actress could always be counted on to come through, especially when a healthy dose of fun in any form was involved.

Rosemary's brother, Frederick, on the other hand, had finally learned to save his shenanigans for the weekends after having put in a full week's worth of work at their father's company, Woolridge & Sons.

With the death of their older brother—also Vera's

first and, to her mind, one true love—Frederick had become the only male Woolridge heir, and their father impressed upon him the duty to learn every nuance of the family business. In a shocking turn of events, Frederick took his job seriously. In fact, it had taken the lingering stain of a murder investigation—with Frederick as the prime suspect—to convince him a sabbatical was in order.

Rounding out the foursome was Desmond Cooper, Frederick's longtime mate, and Rosemary's childhood crush. She'd given up on the fantasy of Desmond a split second after she'd laid eyes on Andrew Lillywhite, but her husband's untimely death the year before had put Rosemary back on the market. At least, according to anyone who felt the need to comment on the situation—such as her mother and, of course, Vera. While Rosemary still got butterflies in her stomach when she was around Desmond, the thought of becoming romantically involved with a man other than her late husband turned their flight into a swarm that made her stomach ache.

Sunny days, sandy beaches, and exotic cocktails near sparkling waters had sounded far too tempting after the ordeal of clearing Frederick's name, and Rosemary had, for once, thrown caution to the wind and decided to treat herself to a much-needed holiday.

As if her life wasn't complicated enough, there was Detective Inspector Maximilian Whittington back in London to consider. Max, a handsome fellow, and a stalwart friend, had worked closely with Andrew in his private investigating enterprise and then, during Frederick's untimely brush with murder, had stepped in to help clear her brother's name.

While Rosemary had been glad of the help, she was not, as Vera continued to insist, in love with Max. Nor was she, as Vera also continued to insist, the lady who doth protest too much. Max was merely a friend, and even if the idea of a romance with him intrigued her, she considered it best to push those feelings aside. That she could do so was, in Rosemary's estimation, a sign that she wasn't ready.

Falling in love should overwhelm all of a woman's senses, not trigger her common sense. That was how it had happened with Andrew and was now the measure by which she would gauge all such experiences. Not that Rosemary intended to have a great many of them.

"We're finally here, Rosie," Vera squealed at a pitch that could have cut glass. "The Isle of Love, that's what they call Cyprus, you know," she said, her emerald eyes sparkling from beneath a sheaf of inky lashes.

Rosemary cocked an eyebrow at her friend. "Yes, I'm aware of the island's nickname, as you've mentioned it approximately eighty-seven times since we left London."

"It's just so beautiful, I can't stand it," Vera continued as if Rosemary hadn't said a word. "You can almost feel the romance, and we haven't even docked yet."

"There are other things in life besides men, you know."

When Vera smiled, even the sun seemed to dim a little in comparison. "Well, of course, there are, dear one, but none so devilishly interesting."

"Where are Fred and Des, anyway?" Rosemary changed the subject while her eyes roamed the deck in search of her brother's head of golden curls. "What am I saying? Obviously, we'll find them—"

"Guzzling down cocktails," Vera finished for her. "And I imagine poor Anna is still in the loo, sicking up." Rosemary's maid had battled motion sickness ever since they'd boarded the train in London and had turned an ugly shade of green before the ship had even pulled completely away from the dock.

"Poor girl. She might have mentioned she didn't travel well," Rosemary said, a note of worry in her voice.

"I expect she was overcome by the excitement of a holiday. She'll come right once her feet are back on solid ground, though I do wonder if she'll spend the entire holiday dreading the return trip."

Rosemary sighed. "Or trying to talk the fair Cecily into hiring her on to avoid it."

"Speaking of, how well do you know this Cecily DeVant person?" Vera asked.

"Not at all, really. She hasn't visited England since I was quite young, and I hardly remember the occasion. Still, as many times as I have listened to Mother wax on about her oldest and dearest friend, I feel as if I know her."

Gripping the rail, Vera raised her face and leaned into the wind. "What's her story?" she said as the breeze ruffled her hair. "How did she come to be running a hotel in Cyprus, of all places?"

Those details hadn't been as important to Rosemary's mother as passing along what she perceived as pertinent facts about the hotel.

"No idea, really. All I know is that whoever built the hotel went to great expense to make it as lavish as possible."

Rosemary watched with a hand at the ready to catch her friend should Vera lean too far.

"I'd have been happy to stay in any sort of place. Travel is meant to broaden one's experience, after all."

Rosemary grinned. "Oh, I daresay you'll appreciate the finer amenities on offer at the Aphrodite Sands. Mother positively gushed over the lift of all things. According to Cecily, it was a task of great endurance and expense to have it shipped over and installed. I'm certain it couldn't have taken as long as it did for Mother to tell the story."

"So long as there's sand, sun, and good gin, I can't imagine we'll lack for anything." Taking Rosemary by the arm, Vera turned away from the rail and the view.

"Now," she continued, "I estimate we have another ten minutes, which leaves just enough time for one last mimosa, don't you think?"

"Lead on, but for heaven's sake, Vera, don't go that way." Having spied three elderly women arguing over deck chairs to her left, Rosemary dragged Vera on a circuitous route to the bar. Halfway through the first day of their voyage, Mrs. Edina Haversham had discovered Vera sunning herself on the forward deck and attached herself like a leech to her favorite actress.

At every turn, she and two other fluffy dowagers sprang out of nowhere, demanding Vera recite lines from one play or another.

"Your flock of admirers will see us and ask you to perform again. We'll never get our mimosa, and I don't think I could take another dramatic death scene reenactment."

"Why, Rosemary darling, I'm positively gutted. Did you not say my Desdemona was a revelation?" Vera's eyes twinkled with great humor.

"And so it was," Rosemary said with a grin. "The first time. Alas, with numerous repetitions, I find

Desdemona pales."

Having avoided the old biddies, the pair strolled over to where Frederick and Desmond held court at the bar. Vera ordered and handed a frothy yellow drink to her friend and took a satisfying sip of her own. "These are going to be dangerous," she mused, elbowing Frederick sharply for no real reason other than to interrupt the boastful story he'd been telling the two attractive women who were hanging on his every word.

"...and then, I punched him square in the jaw—ouch!" he said, turning to Vera in surprise. "What was that for?" he asked, his voice at a slightly higher pitch than normal.

"Oh, you know. Nothing in particular." Vera's eyes sparkled prettily but with razor-sharpness. She linked arms with Rosemary and walked back towards a pair of deck chairs. "He's going to get what's coming to him, that I can promise."

"When he least expects it, I'm certain," Rosemary said with a wry smile. She was used to playing referee between her brother and her best friend, whose relationship was forever fraught with conflict. Desmond had nearly got his head bitten off on the train when he posited the opinion that the constant bickering smelled of romantic interest. Now, as Rosemary met his eyes across the deck, she knew his amused expression meant he was even more convinced of the notion than ever before. "At least this time, you have a good reason for knocking him down a peg or two."

"Darned right I do," Vera agreed, recalling the moment when she and Frederick had been called upon to distract the attention of a group of corrupt gamblers. Given no further order than to create a diversion, Frederick had chosen to run his hand over her backside. His ploy, though ill-advised, had done the trick. Outraged, Vera had kicked up a fuss, but even now, she flushed at the memory of how his hand had felt on her.

"I know it was part of the covert affair and that we took down a notorious criminal as a result, but did he really have to manhandle me to successfully create a distraction? That's right, he did not." She answered her own question before Rosemary could take a breath. "Oh look, we're docking!" All thoughts of revenge seemed to evaporate as the boat came to a stop.

A flurry of activity on the dock from several men in crisp white shirts reminded Rosemary of a glass-encased ant farm she'd seen at a museum when she was a child. In the short time it took to disembark, each one had amassed a pile of luggage from belowdecks and loaded it into the small bus that would take travelers to the hotel.

"Mrs. Woolridge," the driver, a snazzily dressed young man, stuttered in a British accent as Rosemary approached.

"Mrs. Woolridge is my mother," Rosemary

replied with a half smile. "I'm Rosemary Lillywhite, and this lot is with me." She gestured towards her friends.

The boy—for he was barely more than sixteen years old by Rosemary's estimation—turned a deep shade of red and apologized profusely. "I'm so sorry, madam. So sorry. Please accept my deepest apologies."

"It's quite all right, Eustis," she said, peering at the gold-trimmed name badge pinned somewhat awkwardly onto his shirt. "No harm done. You'll find we're an easygoing lot, save my brother, the troublemaker, but I'll tip you handsomely at the end of the trip if you ignore him completely." She winked, and young Eustis sighed with relief.

The bus ride to the hotel was long, dusty, and more than a little jarring, given the condition of the road, which went unnoticed as the scenery commanded the attention of the group.

Groves of citrus and ripening olive trees, their trunks a fascination of twisting shapes, flanked parts of the road from the village, the scent of oranges and lemons riding the warm air like a blessing. There was, Rosemary noted, far more trees than buildings, yet she wouldn't describe the landscape as primitive or untamed.

Eustis kept up a running commentary that Rosemary let flow past her without listening too closely. Her artist's eye was too busy making impressions and memorizing shapes and colors to be turned into sketches later. Locals in traditional garb blended with Brits wearing current fashions to create a wealth of pattern and movement.

Vera, of course, concentrated on the male population, while Frederick kept his eye on the female. Desmond, as was his way, said very little.

Over the crest of a low hill, the Aphrodite Sands Hotel finally came into view, its whitewashed facade and modern architecture standing out in stark contrast to everything they'd seen along the way. With bated breath, the foursome emerged from the bus and approached the front entrance. Stone steps cut into perfect rectangles and buffed to a gleaming shine spanned the width of the hotel, potted ferns and colorful plants dotting the expanse.

Rosemary fingered a rubbery leaf and bent her head to sniff the single flower blossoming from one of its tendrils. Yes, she was going to have a nice, relaxing holiday surrounded by the type of exotic beauty London simply couldn't boast. She only wished she'd packed some canvas and her paints but settled instead to committing the scene to memory.

She trailed behind her companions, who hadn't taken the time to stop and soak in the atmosphere, and approached the front counter at the rear of the group. Vera shot her a look from beneath furrowed brows as the receptionist, a petite, pinch-faced Greek woman with curly black hair, leafed through a leather-bound register.

"I'm sorry," she said, not sounding sorry at all, "but I can only seem to find two rooms listed under the name Woolridge."

"Try Lillywhite," Rosemary said, pushing between Frederick and Vera.

Rosemary's jovial mood plummeted while the receptionist scanned through the names listed on the page again. "I am sorry. If you would wait one moment," she said, and without any explanation, turned and strode away. After a few minutes, she returned with another woman in tow.

"Well, I'll be—" The second woman stopped to gaze at Rosemary.

This, Rosemary decided, could be none other than Cecily DeVant. It wasn't the English accent or the familiarity with which the woman spoke that created such certainty; it was the description that her mother had given Rosemary before she left London. When Evelyn Woolridge had said her friend was the 'oddest looking woman' she'd ever met, Rosemary had taken the statement with a grain of salt.

Evelyn still couldn't wrap her mind around why not all women focused on their looks or aspired to greater heights than marrying well, so her perspective tended to be somewhat one-dimensional.

However, in this instance, it seemed her mother had not missed the mark at all. Cecily's face was a contradiction of angles. Impossibly high cheekbones created a triangular effect between her eyes and mouth, the features as symmetrical as those of an Egyptian princess. That was if you could look beyond the prominent, arrow-straight nose that angled towards the left side of her face so abruptly it gave Rosemary a start.

"You must be Rosemary," she trilled, stepping forward with her arms outstretched. "You're the spitting image of your mother when she was a girl. It's striking, as a matter of fact," Cecily said, cocking her head to one side as she made her appraisal.

"Yes," Rosemary smiled. She couldn't help but take an instant liking to the woman, though her mother had mentioned getting on Cecily's bad side was inadvisable, and Rosemary had no doubt the statement was true. Formidable, be she friend or foe, was a fitting word for Cecily DeVant. "You must be Cecily. It's a pleasure to meet you again." Rosemary held out a hand but was instead enveloped in a lavender-scented embrace.

"We'll have to take lunch together sometime during your stay. I have many stories about your mother I think you'll find amusing," Cecily said, her gaze having come upon Frederick during the conversation. "And you look too much like your father not to be Cecil's son." He was treated to an enthusiastic hug, which he returned in kind.

"Cecil and Cecily," he said, grinning and shaking his head. "I can only imagine how confusing that was for Mother."

Cecily laughed. "Perhaps, though the only thing I ever heard her call your father was 'darling' or 'dear' or some other such term of endearment. Are they still as besotted with each other as they once were?"

Rosemary detected a hint of jealousy in Cecily's tone, not that she could blame her. It wasn't easy being a third wheel, as Rosemary had learned since becoming a single woman for the second time in her life.

Frederick assured her that their parents were still happily married and then introduced Cecily to Vera and Desmond. Once pleasantries had been exchanged to her satisfaction, she retreated to the other side of the counter and took a look at the ledger.

"Gloria, honestly!" Cecily admonished the receptionist, whose face went a deep shade of scarlet. "Could I have made it any easier for you to reserve the proper number of rooms? I distinctly remember writing you a note explaining that the Woolridge-Lillywhite party would need two suites plus a room for their staff. That's three rooms, and you only reserved two," she continued, even though the public shaming of an employee made everyone feel somewhat uncomfortable. Anna hung back, a look of pure mortification on her round little face.

"I'm sorry." Gloria dropped her eyes, but not

before Rosemary detected mutiny in her expression. "Margaret saw the note and passed the information along to me, but one of us must have made a mistake. All the suites are filled. Should I ask one of the other guests to change rooms?"

Desmond stepped forward and cleared his throat loudly. "No need to trouble yourself, really. Frederick and I will do just as well in the smaller room." He received a nod from Rosemary and a small, grateful smile from the receptionist, who peered at him with interest.

"Yes," Rosemary said, "and Anna will stay in our suite, right, Vera?" Vera nodded her agreement.

"Very well, but your graciousness doesn't let Gloria off the hook." Cecily continued to berate the woman, whose face had gone stony. Her eyes brimmed with unshed tears.

"You're lucky I don't let you go, Gloria." Cecily's tone insinuated this wasn't the first such mistake the girl had made. "We'll discuss this further later." She took her leave, citing urgent hotel business, and Gloria breathed a sigh of relief at her departure.

Rosemary thought once more how her mother had been right—one certainly didn't want to get on Cecily DeVant's bad side.